Praise for *The Miracle:*

"L'Heureux's snappy, succulent novel of faith and body, starts out sharp and ends with a razor slash. Lean, crisp prose delineates Father LeBlanc's quest to be a good priest and the faith-sustaining events that propel him there." —*The Baltimore Sun*

"[A] profound, gentle novel . . . Measures up here to [L'Heureux's] best storytelling. This novel is darkly funny and lightly told." —*San Jose Mercury News*

"Mr. L'Heureux's timely—and risky—attempt to put a human face on religious aspirations, limitations and belief could not be more brave, or, as it turns out, more rewarding. . . . This powerful book may be Mr. L'Heureux's finest." —*Washington Times*

"L'Heureux brings the priest [in *The Miracle*] through his crisis of faith with the same tenderness that makes all his books such a pleasure to read." —*Los Angeles Times Book Review*

"Engaging and thought-provoking." —*Christian Century*

"A wry but revelatory look at the connection between faith and love . . . L'Heureux's strength is his ability to expose the all-too-human foibles and flaws of his outstanding ensemble cast, as he connects the dots with short, punchy scenes that instantly get to the heart of the matter. As usual, L'Heureux also looks unflinchingly at a variety of tough moral issues, balancing the serious stuff with humor in a deceptively light style that makes this book entertaining as well as challenging." —*Publishers Weekly* (starred review)

"A finely crafted story of a young priest's crisis of faith (and love) is [L'Heureux's] latest success. . . . Deeply moving and personal, told with great restraint and skill."    —*Kirkus Reviews* (starred review)

"There is great humanity in this well-crafted story, expressed largely through the appealing characters of priests, and a final message: choose life."                                        —*Booklist*

# THE MIRACLE

# THE MIRACLE

*a novel by*

# JOHN

# L'HEUREUX

Grove Press
New York

*Published simultaneously in Canada*
*Printed in the United States of America*

FIRST GROVE PRESS EDITION

Library of Congress Cataloging-in-Publication Data

L'Heureux, John.
    The miracle : a novel / by John L'Heureux.
        p. cm.
    ISBN 0-8021-4026-2 (pbk.)
    1. Clergy—Fiction.   2. Miracles—Fiction.   3. Massachusetts—Fiction.
4. Seaside resorts—Fiction.   I. Title.

PS3562.H4 M47 2002
813'.54—dc21                                                            2002016413


Design by Laura Hammond Hough


Grove Press

841 Broadway

New York, NY 10003

03 04 05 06 07   10 9 8 7 6 5 4 3 2 1

*FOR JOAN*

"Choose life."

Deuteronomy 30:19

# THE MIRACLE

# ONE

AT THIS TIME—IT IS THE EARLY 1970S—FATHER PAUL LeBlanc is still an ordinary parish priest in South Boston, a huge Irish ghetto that stretches from the Southeast Expressway down to Quincy and out to the coast. South Boston is very Catholic, with four different parishes and thirteen priests, and St. Matthew's parish, where Father LeBlanc is stationed, is the most Irish of them all. This is a neighborhood of spruced-up three-deckers—gray and white and tan—with some wood and brick two-deckers, and a few single-family houses with driveways. No matter the color of the houses, they all seem gray when you stand at the corner and look down the street. It is a gray parish. There are a lot of Irish bars—McGillicuddy's, Ahern's, Matt Doherty's—and even the 7-Eleven is run by a guy they call Maloney. Actually he is Italian, and his name is Meloni, but it sounds Irish when you say it. So. All the cops are from South Boston, and so are the firemen, and if you own a grocery store or a drugstore or a beauty shop in the parish, most likely you live there. Most people work at Gilette or city hall or one of the utility companies. Nobody has money and everybody has something they are after, a better job or an education for their kids or a house of their own with a front yard and a backyard. Unlike the hippies who spend their time lying down in the street to protest the war in Vietnam, everybody here in St. Matthews works and expects to go on working. Father LeBlanc loves the place and he loves being a priest. There are no miracles in his life except the ordinary ones—waking, eating, speaking, sleeping—and he doesn't aspire to miracles. He just wants to be a good man and a good priest and, mostly, he keeps out of trouble.

Mostly, because in fact he is often in trouble, though not serious enough trouble to get himself exiled. He has protested against the war in Vietnam, as most of the priests do, but it is the way he did it that was bad: at Sunday mass, during the Prayer of the Faithful, he said—it just came to him, he didn't plan it—"Let us pray that our Lord will forgive our country the murders we commit each new day in Vietnam," and the congregation responded, haltingly, "Let us pray to the Lord." The phone rang all afternoon as parishioners with sons in Vietnam called to complain. Father LeBlanc was summoned to the pastor's office and, after a long lecture on common sense and moral responsibility, Father Mackin asked him, please, to *think* about what he was going to say before he said it. On the following Sunday, Father LeBlanc apologized from the pulpit. That was a bad moment.

And he has taught religion to seniors at the high school until rumors got back to the principal that he had "slighted" the doctrine of papal infallibility and "implied" that masturbation was not a sin. What he actually said was "Yeah, sure, the pope is infallible, but only when he speaks from the chair of Peter. That's a folding chair, by the way." And of masturbation he wondered aloud, "It's a mortal sin? Hmmmm. An interesting question." After that he was assigned to teach Latin.

And once, but only once, he said mass using a loaf of wheat bread and Gallo wine for the consecration. It was a private mass for a group of nuns he studied with at Boston College, and one of them wrote home about it, and her mother mentioned it to a friend of the family, and, in short, it took only a week before Father LeBlanc was in serious trouble.

So he stands warned: priests like him get transferred every day. Next stop, the boonies. He is a wild priest, a troublesome priest, and it is only a matter of time until he is dealt with.

†

To the parishioners—except to the ones who have sons and daughters in Vietnam—Father LeBlanc is a wild priest but a good one. He is handsome and young and not exactly sexy, but strong. He is a guy who is full of energy and life, and it is always exciting to be with him because he knows how to relate to people. He is friendly and normal. He is funny. There is nothing queer about him, the way there sometimes is about priests who wear that cassock all the time.

Father LeBlanc is just like anybody from the parish, except he is smarter and he teaches Latin at the high school and he is a priest. You have to remind yourself he is a priest when you see him in his sweats playing basketball with the kids because he is built so great and he can be a mean son of a bitch under the net when he goes up for a hook shot. He always says, "Shit" when he misses an easy shot, and then he says, "Sorry." He never uses the "F" word.

He is smart, energetic, filled with life. A parishioner would look at him and think, Here is somebody who has given it all up, and yet he is happy. He is happier than anybody. Look how he gets along with the kids. Look how he always has a smile and that lift to his step. You can tell him anything in confession because he is very broad-minded about sex and birth control. He jogs every morning. He even sings popular songs, not very well, but he tries. He is what the modern Church ought to be. They think.

†

3

Father LeBlanc knows they think he is a wild priest, and sometimes he is pleased that they do. It makes him interesting. When he catches himself thinking this way, though, he is ashamed of such petty vanity, and he prays against smallness and pride and the stupidity of caring what people think. What matters is sacrifice. What matters is to obliterate the self.

†

"St. Matthew's is a very busy parish. It's an old-fashioned parish, the people are devout, they don't want their faith being upset by new ideas."

Father Mackin, the pastor, says this at the dinner table, generally, not to anybody in particular. Father Boyle and Father LeBlanc listen dutifully, so Father Mackin continues. "We still have people going to confession," he says, "as you both know. And that's a wonderful thing in this day and age."

"Huh," Father Boyle says, not looking up. Father Boyle always has a drink before dinner and tonight he has had several.

Father LeBlanc nods agreement, deciding it is wiser to say nothing. He is the youngest priest in the parish, and everybody likes a young priest except the older ones. He knows that.

"What is this stuff we're eating?" Father Boyle asks.

"I think it's lamb," Father Mackin says, just as Father LeBlanc says, "I think it's veal."

"I'll tell you what it is," Father Boyle said. "It's a goddamn rubber boot."

They laugh at that, and then Father Mackin says, "What do you think, Paul?"

"It does have a boot kind of taste." Father LeBlanc pokes the meat with his fork.

"No, I mean what do you think about the parish? It's a traditional parish, St. Matthew's. And new ideas upset people."

"Oh yeah. We ought to stamp out new ideas."

Which ends conversation at that particular dinner.

Father LeBlanc, as usual, is penitent. Poor old Mackin is a wonderful man, patient, a devoted priest. And Boyle is a good man, too, even though he has this drinking problem. Why can't he give them a break?

Father LeBlanc changes into his sweats and goes over to the school gym, where he pumps iron until he aches all over. He showers, singing all the big numbers from *Gypsy,* and then he pops into church and prays for the gift of restraint.

†

Father LeBlanc is at ease with everybody. He celebrates mass, he hears confessions, he teaches his Latin class at the high school—last year Virgil, this year Ovid—and he visits hospitals and the prison and the homes of parishioners who are sick or shut in. Sometimes he plays basketball with the kids after school, and sometimes he just hangs out at the parish hall where he is famous for his imitations of Jimmy Durante and Ethel Merman and Perry Como, all those old-timers.

Life at St. Matthew's is great. The parishioners are always glad to see you, and they are good hardworking people, and deeply religious in their way, once you get to know them one-on-one. When they are in trouble, for instance. A death in the family. A divorce. That's when he can see that they want something more. They long for the same thing he longs for. And he has no doubt that this is the longing for God. They are good people because they aspire to be good people. He loves them. He loves this parish. He is comfortable everywhere, except in the rectory itself.

†

Father Mackin, the pastor, is new to the parish, a man in his sixties. He has taught philosophy at the seminary for almost thirty years, and he regards this parish as his reward for all those years of service. Also, his kind of philosophy—Thomistic—holds less interest for seminarians these days. They prefer just the basics. In fact, the bishop has sent Father Mackin here to tighten things up. There is too much talk among parishioners about the "role of the laity" and "parish councils" and too much interference in how the church is run. Father Mackin is known to hold traditional, reliable views. He is prudent, kind, and patient. He knows how to handle Boyle and LeBlanc, the two impossible curates.

Father Boyle is in his fifties, morbidly thin, with a gray face and an air of defeat. He has a little thatch of short gray hair that is never combed, and he wears a cassock that is never clean. He looks like what he is, a confirmed alcoholic. Father Boyle has spent most of his priestly life at St. Matthew's, and the parishioners are used to him and accept his little problem with drink. He is human, weak. What can you do about a man like that except, of course, pray for him?

Father LeBlanc is another matter. He is young and energetic, and that is good, within limits. It is always nice to have young priests; it shows that the Church is up-to-date. But LeBlanc has had one of those left-wing Jesuit educations, with a B.A. in classics and an M.A. in social something-or-other, and of course he is addicted to exactly those ideas

Father Mackin has been sent here to crush. Or rather to monitor. Right now there is a growing controversy about busing—sending white kids to black schools and, take your pick, sending black kids to white schools—and the bishop wants his diocese to stay out of it. No preaching, no social apostolate crap. "We've got our own schools to worry about, and busing is not a Catholic problem." And then he added, "We don't expect miracles. We just want you to keep the lid on."

Father Mackin reminds himself that Father LeBlanc is a good preacher and he is great in the confessional, if you can judge by the number of people waiting for him. God knows he is generous with his time.

Still, look at him. He must be the most extroverted priest in the world; he lives to play sports and perform and . . . what? . . . sing those goddamn songs. He is good-looking, no question, and he is popular with adults as well as kids, and—thank God—there has never been a question of drink or women or boys.

But what is he like inside?

Does he have any interior life at all?

†

Father LeBlanc has an interior life that is secret from everyone and, in some ways, secret from himself. All the noise—the singing, the basketball, the easy laughter—is merely a cover for what is going on inside.

He worries about hearing confessions. He worries about how he says mass. He worries about his worrying, which is a sign of vanity.

Before mass each morning he kneels straight up at his prie-dieu, his head down, his eyes closed, and he prays not to be such a shit. He is the least profitable of servants. He is a failure, a priest who wants

to please people. Does he want it enough to sell out the Church? Is
that what is going on? Judas betrayed Christ for thirty pieces of silver.
And am I selling kindness in the confessional for a cheap popularity?
He prays for help. He prays to do and say the right thing. He keeps
on praying until he achieves a sense of peace or at least until his mind
goes blank. He is doing the best he can. At least, he wants to do the
best he can.

The thought comes to him: So did Luther.

†

This is not the age of miracles, but Father LeBlanc feels that now
and then miracles do happen in the confessional. The boys come
in and say they used the Lord's name in vain and they missed morning and evening prayers and—they always speed up here—they
masturbated several times and they lied twice and they beat up their
little brother. The old sin sandwich: put the easy stuff at top and
bottom and then slip masturbation into the middle where it might
not be noticed. Father LeBlanc plays along. He tells them yes, it is
hard to remember to say morning and evening prayers, and sometimes you can't help wanting to beat up your little brother, but you
have to concentrate on the positive things and remember what a
nice family you've got and remember how you can help make things
better by not being a grouch all the time or by helping out around
the house or being patient with your folks and not talking back to
them. Your folks are tired. They work hard. So give in a little.
Okay? And, oh yes, something else, you mentioned masturbation.
He pauses so they have time to realize he knows, and then he speeds
up again. Well, try not to let that get important in your life. Sex is
a natural and wonderful thing, and you're still young, with your

8

whole life ahead of you. Thank God you're living such a good life. For your penance say three Hail Marys. And they leave the confessional, these kids, better than they came in. More free to make something of themselves.

It is the same thing with women and birth control, except he meets that problem head-on. "Why do you mention this in confession?" he asks. "Do you feel birth control is sinful?" And then he talks about it slowly, carefully, helping each one realize it is her own conscience she has to live with, not the pope's. Men are easier to deal with, either because they welcome the personal responsibility or because they don't care a hell of a lot but just want to be okay with the Church. But they all go away happy. He is doing the right thing, an important thing. It is what Jesus would do, he is sure.

What bothers him is their conviction that sin is necessarily sexual. They confess the same old things over and over—fornication, adultery, masturbation—and how much of it really matters? He finds it hard to imagine that God is upset when some twelve-year-old jacks off. Who does it hurt? What does it matter? The poor kid is just checking the equipment. Adultery is something else, of course; people get hurt in adultery. Which is why it is sinful: because it violates charity and justice, not just because it is sexual. Nobody seems to care about charity, a nice safe category of sin. They are all quite happy to confess uncharitable thoughts, uncharitable conversations, uncharitable acts. And so he sits there for two hours and listens to the endless catalog of small failures. Of good people. Because only good people come to confession in the first place.

He leaves the confessional happy, filled with energy and life. He sings, mostly on key, "put on a happy face."

†

Sometimes he has to smile to himself, because he knows he is possessed by the demon of discontent. He says outrageous things just to be funny. Or to shock somebody. Or because he has been praying and can't stand himself for another second. When the fit is on him, he can't help himself. He just says it.

Dinnertime is the worst. He doesn't care about food, and for some reason, he cares a lot—during dinner—about social problems. First it was the war and then it was race and now each night he brings up the subject of busing as if it is a parish problem they are all concerned about.

"The parish has no busing problem," Father Mackin says, stabbing at the peas on his plate. He has explained this to Father LeBlanc over and over again. "Parishioners don't like the idea of all these blacks being brought into their neighborhood, of course not. That doesn't mean they're against blacks. We have always had blacks in parochial schools, and some of them are pretty smart—that's how they got accepted, that's how they got scholarship money—and, up until recently, they've always known their place. But everything is getting out of control these days, and people just want to protest. It's becoming a way of life. Protest. Protest. Protest."

Father LeBlanc interrupts with something about democracy and justice, but Father Mackin has had enough. He falls silent with a hostile silence that even Father LeBlanc recognizes.

After dinner Father LeBlanc says he is sorry if he has given offense. Father Mackin nods and says nothing.

†

How can he be so happy in his work and so miserably lonely at the same time? He bursts out laughing because, in his brain, he hears a voice—as clear as the voice of God—saying to him, "Hey! Who cares!"

†

Father Mackin calls Father LeBlanc to his office and says he is disturbed that one of the Christian doctrine teachers has asked if it is true—"as Father LeBlanc says"—that not all methods of birth control are equally bad.

Father LeBlanc doesn't remember saying that, but, he says now, it seems to him that abortion is more extreme than using prophylactics, don't you agree? And then of course there is the rhythm method, which is different from prophylactics in that prophylactics work and rhythm doesn't. And then . . .

Father Mackin shakes his head and explains that it is better not to discuss birth control at all, since the Church's stand on it, though perfectly clear to any rational mind, is so open to misinterpretation by all the others.

"And," he adds, "will you please *stop* singing in the corridors. This is not a rock emporium!"

†

Father LeBlanc can't get it out of his head for days. A rock emporium! And for those days he is careful not to sing in the corridors.

†

Father Mackin says he is distressed to hear the latest: Father LeBlanc has chosen to discuss the issue of busing not only at dinner but in his Latin class at the high school. Several parents have phoned to complain.

"There is no theology of busing. Do not discuss the matter again."

Father LeBlanc smiles a little and looks penitent.

"And Paul? Think about this, if you will. You're getting to be a royal pain in the ass." Father Mackin is losing patience.

†

Father Boyle has been drinking, of course, but he is not drunk, and that is a nice change. He is chatty at dinner, and after dinner he invites Father LeBlanc to his room. Father LeBlanc begs off—he has a funeral mass the next morning and has to prepare a homily—but Father Boyle insists that he needs help. Reluctantly, Father LeBlanc says fine, sure, okay.

Father LeBlanc has been at St. Matthew's for three years, but until now he has never been in Father Boyle's room. He looks around, surprised at the chaos. There is a bed and a bureau and a small television on top of the bureau, but everything else is covered in heaps of paper—newspapers, magazines, advertisements, pages torn from a spiral notebook. There are even letters. Who would be writing to Father Boyle? Next to the television there is a collection of tiny stone animals. There are several full ashtrays. There are books everywhere. By the look of the place, Father Boyle must have started accumulating this stuff long before he took to the bottle.

"Well," Father LeBlanc says, looking around for a seat. "Lots of books."

Father Boyle scoots a pile of papers off the easy chair for Father LeBlanc and then sits behind his desk and tilts back his chair. After a moment, he says, "Do you mind if I have a drink?"

Father LeBlanc makes a gesture, palm up: be my guest.

"You?"

Father LeBlanc shakes his head no.

"I want to know about confessions," Father Boyle says. "I want to know how you do it."

"Do what? Is this the birth-control business again?"

"As a matter of fact."

"And is this entrapment?" He goes red, which surprises him, and he goes redder still.

"I'm sincere about this." Father Boyle stares across his glass, and Father LeBlanc thinks, Yes, he is sober after all.

"Okay. Fine. Sure. I'd be happy to talk about it sometime. Right now maybe isn't the best time."

"Why not? Because I'm drunk and wouldn't understand? Try me."

"Oh, I didn't mean . . ." Father LeBlanc begins.

"Yes, you did. You do."

And then, doubting he should do this but unable to stop himself, Father LeBlanc explains the process of reasoning by which he helps "concerned Catholics to form their own consciences in an intelligent and responsible way, in the light of Vatican II." He uses these exact words, part of his confessional lecture. "You see the difference?" he asks. "It's not advocating birth control. It's advocating responsibility. It's about the primacy of conscience."

"But how do you actually do it?" Father Boyle asks. "What do you actually say?"

"You just help them see where *they* feel their duty lies. It's *their* conscience, after all."

"But how do you get them to see it? What do you tell them?"

Father LeBlanc gives Father Boyle a long hard look. Is he, in fact, drunk? Is he sincere? Or is Boyle getting the goods on him so that he can stagger off to the pastor, or even to the bishop, to cause all kinds of trouble?

"You could help me," Father Boyle says. "Sincerely."

Father LeBlanc clears his throat and thinks about it. This could be very dumb. There is nothing Rome likes better than slapping down the uppity parish priest. And all you have to do to get branded "uppity" is mention married clergy or women priests or—bingo—birth control.

"I think I'm coming down with a cold," Father LeBlanc says. "Help me."

Oh God, Father LeBlanc thinks, and plunges ahead. "I do this. First off, I talk to them about the other things they've mentioned—you know, the usual stuff, impatience with their kids, missing mass, sins against charity, stuff like that. And after I've talked for a while, I say something like—let's see—'I think you mentioned that you've been practicing birth control? Is that right?' And they'll say they use the pill, or they've been trying to stop, or they know it's a sin. But the thing is to ask them, right away, why they think it's a sin, and invariably they'll answer: 'Because the Church says it is.'"

"And then?"

"And then I try to explain that it isn't just a question of what the Church says. The birth-control issue is far more complicated than that."

"But what do you *say*?"

"Oh God. I *say* that, yes, the Church sets down as a general rule—and I underline those words for them: *as a general rule*—that Catholics shouldn't practice birth control. But the issue, I tell them, is essentially a personal one, involving private rather than general norms of morality, and so it's the responsibility of each of us to *in-*

form our minds on the matter so that we can properly *form* our own *consciences*. You see, I've got it down to a rote speech, practically."

Father Boyle drains his glass and pours another drink, straight Scotch this time. He leans forward. "And then you help them inform their minds?"

"I tell them they should ask themselves three questions. Like this. I say: 'First, you should ask yourself if you are shirking your Christian responsibilities; that is to say, "Do I just want the pleasures of sex without the responsibility of children?" Now, you've already got two children, you said, so obviously you're not out just for pleasure.' Or, if they don't have any children, I say, 'Probably you'll want to have children later, someday.' Anyway, I take away their worry about the sex part. Then I say, 'Second, you ask yourself if there is some real *need* for you to use birth control. But you've already indicated financial reasons—or psychological, or physical, or whatever.' I just fit the answer to the case, you see. Then, 'Third, you should ask yourself if this is going to help you and your spouse to lead a fuller, happier, more responsible Christian life. Now, only you and your spouse together can answer that, so you should have a discussion with him or her, and then once you've made up your mind to use or not to use birth control, then just go ahead and live comfortably with your decision. And whatever you do, don't mention it in confession again, because eventually you're sure to run into some crazy priest who'll scream and yell and say you're committing mortal sin.'"

"Some crazy priest."

"Well . . ."

"Fantastic."

"Well, it's sound morality, I think. And it helps people to assume responsibility for their own lives." Father LeBlanc pauses a moment and then adds, "I try to get them past fear, past blind obedience." He pauses once more. "I try to help them see it's only love that matters."

Father Boyle says nothing. He stares past Father LeBlanc with a surprised look on his face. Father LeBlanc turns, expecting to see Father Mackin, expecting to be denounced for hypocrisy or heresy or God knows what. But no one is there. Father Boyle is merely looking into a new world of possibilities.

"Again. Say it all again," Father Boyle says. "I want to get those three points by heart." He pours himself another glass of Scotch, and before Father LeBlanc can continue his explanation, Father Boyle looks up and mutters, "I always wanted to be a good priest," and a boozy tear slides down his cheek.

†

Father LeBlanc lies in bed looking out at the moon. It is three months before he will be sent into exile at the beach in New Hampshire, and he is still at St. Matthew's in Boston. Nonetheless, even in this paradise of the priesthood, he is anguished, he is unloved and unloving, he is hungry. He has vowed his life and his mind and his body to the service of Jesus Christ, and he does the best he is able, but . . . does he?

He is alone. Abandoned. He feels nothing.

He reaches beneath the blankets and touches himself. He masturbates, without a fantasy, without an image. He is thinking of nothing. He is fucking nothing. It is all nothing. It is all hopeless.

The next morning before mass he seeks out Father Boyle and confesses that he has masturbated. Why is masturbation a sin for him but not for the kids he counsels in confession? He has no idea.

They are free. He isn't.

†

Father LeBlanc has been summoned to the Kremlin, which is what they call the bishop's residence in Boston. It is an old brownstone mansion crammed with antique furniture and Persian carpets and dusty portraits of dead or dying bishops. To be summoned here means serious trouble. They have provided him with a long list of questions about faith and morals, and he has responded to each in writing. Today he will be examined by a monsignor assigned to his case. The procedure is straight out of the sixteenth century.

Now he sits across the desk from Monsignor Glynn, who turns out to be a nice old man, lean and red-faced, with white hair like a bird's nest. He wears wire-rimmed glasses that slip down his nose and make him look like a bright child. It's easy to be deceived, though. Some of these old guys have a mind like a razor and a tongue to go with it.

"Ed Glynn's my name," he says. "You're Paul LeBlanc?"

"Yes, Monsignor. Um, yes."

"Have a hard candy? I'm trying to stop smoking."

Father LeBlanc smiles and shakes his head no as Monsignor Glynn pops a candy into his own mouth.

"You're a very smart young man," Monsignor Glynn says, shifting the hard candy to one side of his mouth. He indicates the papers in front of him. "These answers are fine, very thoughtful. I admire the way you've quoted Vatican II in the questions on conscience. Very fine." He crunches the hard candy, swallows, and then they talk for a long while about birth control and individual conscience and the confessional. At the end the monsignor indicates there have been complaints about Father LeBlanc's position on birth control, but "like Pilate with Jesus, I find no fault in you," he says. They both laugh at this, and Monsignor Glynn pushes the papers aside and leans back. "Tell me," he says. "Quite apart from your 'case'—which will be fine, by the way, you seem harmless enough to me—I'm curious to know what you think about sin. Off the record. Just between us. Do you think that *anything* is sinful?" Father LeBlanc looks at him as if to say of course. "What?" Monsignor Glynn asks. "What exactly?"

"Off the record? Just between us?"

"Between us."

Father LeBlanc is exhilarated suddenly. "I think it was a mistake for the Church to get into the sex business in the first place. There's no evidence that Jesus was upset about prostitutes or homosexuals or even the woman taken in adultery."

"You don't think adultery is wrong?"

"Of course it's wrong, but not because it's sexual. It's wrong because it's a sin against justice. And, for that matter, against charity as well."

"Charity and justice. You're quick on your feet."

"But isn't it?"

"Indeed."

"If the Church took charity and justice as seriously as it takes masturbation and birth control, it would be a very different Church."

"So the Church is the problem."

There is silence and a clock ticks somewhere.

"No, I'm the problem. I know that."

"Yes," Monsignor Glynn says.

"I don't know what's wrong with me."

They say nothing for some time, and then Monsignor Glynn asks, "What do you want? Deep down, what?"

"I want to be a good man," he says, "and a good priest."

Monsignor Glynn looks at him.

"And I try to love God."

"But you don't let him in, do you." It is not a question. "Why not let him in?"

Suddenly the interview is over, and Monsignor Glynn stands up. "There's a man you should meet, an old friend of mine, Tom Moriarty. He's the pastor of a little beach parish in New Hampshire. You'd like him. He talks like you. He thinks like you. Except he's a saint." He comes around the desk to shake Father LeBlanc's hand and give him his blessing, but just as he leans forward to embrace him, Father LeBlanc turns toward the door. It is an awkward, impossible moment.

"I'll see you before long," Monsignor Glynn says.

So perhaps there has been a miracle and he will not be transferred after all.

†

Two days later the bishop's secretary phones Father Mackin, who summons Father LeBlanc to his office and says he is about to be transferred. To a lovely beach parish in New Hampshire. Our Lady of Victories. Father LeBlanc goes white for a moment, and blinks, and says, "Thank you, Father." But on the way back to his room, he knocks on Father Boyle's door. There is a long silence and the clink of a bottle against glass. Father LeBlanc knocks again and pushes the door open.

"Are you the one?" Father LeBlanc leans into Father Boyle's room. "Are you the one who turned me in?"

Father Boyle is drunk, however, and does not understand what Father LeBlanc is talking about.

"I'm leaving St. Matthew's. I'm being sent to Our Lady of Victories. In New Hampshire!"

Father Boyle shifts in his chair, shakes his head, concentrates. His eyes are wide, crazy. And then he smiles, beautifully. "You're Jesus Christ," he says.

Father LeBlanc starts as if he has been slapped. He steps outside the door and closes it. Then he thinks of Monsignor Glynn and opens the door and asks Father Boyle the question the monsignor has asked him.

"But you don't let him in. Do you?"

"Who?"

"Jesus Christ."

"Yes!" Father Boyle says emphatically. "Tha's why I drink."

Father LeBlanc closes the door before he realizes what Father Boyle meant.

†

A week later Father LeBlanc gets a letter from the bishop confirming what he already knows. He is to be transferred to Our Lady of Victories parish in New Hampshire. At once. He will assist Father Thomas Francis Moriarty, who is ill.

So the miracle has not occurred after all.

He goes to his room and, mad as hell, kneels down to say a prayer for Monsignor Glynn. Then he goes out to throw some hoops. He is angry and disappointed for the rest of the day, unaware that the whole time he is packing his bags, he is humming "Everything's Comin' Up Roses."

# TWO

FATHER LEBLANC IS IN HIS SECOND YEAR AT OUR
Lady of Victories in New Hampshire. The Vietnam War is winding
down, the campus revolutions have subsided, and the schoolkids in
Boston are being bused back and forth around the city. Everybody
has got what he wants and everybody is miserable. Father LeBlanc
has missed it all. No matter. This is God's will.

It is very hot, a June day with no breeze at all, not even here
by the ocean. The gulls are silent, and in the distance the waves make
only a hissing sound. The honeysuckle sweetness in the air makes it
difficult even to breathe. Nonetheless, in his tiny, suffocating room
Father LeBlanc kneels in prayer, his cassock buttoned tight to the
neck. He clenches his hands until his knuckles shine with the effort,
but he does not lean against the prie-dieu. He kneels straight up,
without support, because kneeling this way is harder and therefore
perhaps better or more meritorious, even though merit is not on his
mind just now. Hope is on his mind. And despair.

Since coming to New Hampshire, Father LeBlanc has read
many books about priests; with each he has asked himself, "Is it I,
Lord?" He has read about the priest who loves God but not people.
The priest whose pride must be humbled. The priest who discov-
ers virtue only when he discovers that he himself is a sinner. Father
LeBlanc has read Bernanos and Mauriac and Greene, so he knows

all about these priests. And, worse still, he has read the newspapers and *Time* magazine and *Newsweek,* so he knows the variety of public and personal humiliations available to priests. Alcoholism, first of all. And then sex: with women in the parish, with women of the night, with women who come in to clean or cook or take dictation. And sex with children. With little girls who are the daughters of old friends. Or with altar boys or boys on camping trips or boys who are runaways and need a place to sleep for the night. It's molestation, regardless of the sex of the child, and it's in the newspapers all the time. It is horrible, unspeakable. He does not want to be tested in this kind of fire. He gives thanks that the days are past when God took you seriously and gave you boils all over your body and took away your wife and your kids and your camels and left you on a dung heap. These days you're on your own. Still, you can't choose how you'll be tested.

Father LeBlanc spends his morning meditation—not only this morning but every morning—contemplating what it means to be a good man and a good priest. He is trying to extinguish the self. He tries not to sing in the corridors. He tries to be a happy priest but not a boisterous one. He tries to get rid of everything, anything, that calls attention to himself. He wants to make the ultimate sacrifice and cease to exist.

He thinks this—he must cease to exist—and at the same time he wonders: what is the point of existence if you're merely going to crush it out? And then he asks forgiveness for such thoughts.

Father LeBlanc understands that God has gone to great lengths to get his attention, shipping him out of Boston, out of *life* almost, and landing him in this godforsaken beach town where nothing ever happens. But he has taken the transfer seriously and he has tried for almost two years now to respond. But God is on vacation, apparently, and left the Muzak playing. Hello? Hello? He's tried hard, he's prayed a lot, he's given up everything. He's been obedient and chaste and poor. He flagellates himself secretly. Nothing works. So he is praying for hope.

He is thirty-four and very young to have run out of hope, but there you are. Is this what comes of being a troublesome priest?

The sweat trickles down his face and he does not brush it away. It soaks his T-shirt under the arms. It makes his crotch itchy. Nor does he brush away the fly that buzzes about him, waiting to land. This is all part of getting through the day.

It is 7:30 A.M. and he is making his morning meditation before the day gets started. His back hurts and his knees hurt and his mind wanders for a moment, and now he is back in Boston in the confessional box. A woman has just confessed to practicing birth control—about the tenth one that afternoon—and he asks her why she mentions this in confession. "Because it's a sin," she says, "because the pope says you can't." "Well, it's a matter of conscience," he says, "and the pope has decided he won't practice birth control, but now you have to make your own decision." She gasps, and then she laughs a little, and he laughs a little and says, "That's terrible. I shouldn't have said that. I was making light of a serious matter and I shouldn't."

He loved moments like that, and he knows it's exactly that smart-ass kind of thing he's got to stamp out.

Still, he would like to be back in South Boston, dealing with the working poor and the homeless and, goddammit, *doing* something. He has a degree in classics and another in social science; he has worked two years in the slums and three more at St. Matthew's; this is the work he does best. But he is not doing it. Instead—and he has obeyed, he is obedient—he has been sent to a rich parish at the beach. Our Lady of Victories. In New Hampshire.

†

Across the hall Father Moriarty lies in bed waiting for Rose to bring his breakfast.

"Rose, goddammit," he shouts, "where the hell is my breakfast!" Father Moriarty shouts for a number of reasons. It proves he is still alive. And it's sure to bother Father LeBlanc, who is trying to meditate. And it may get Rose to move her behind. In his thinking, these are all good and desirable things.

"Roh-oh-oh-se," he shouts, and he imagines Father LeBlanc shifting uneasily on his kneeler. Handsome LeBlanc, with all that black wavy hair and those teeth and with no sense of humor whatsoever. Truly, God is the ultimate joker. He gave Father LeBlanc those boyish good looks, that splendid body, when all he wants is to be a saint. Father Moriarty had diagnosed sanctity as LeBlanc's problem within the first week of his arrival. And here I'm the one who's a saint, he thinks, with a body that's becoming my coffin.

He smiles at the idea of being a saint and he yells louder than ever, "Rose, darling girl, where is my goddamn breakfast!"

Father Moriarty has ALS, which the nurse calls Lou Gehrig's disease, though he himself calls it amyotrophic lateral sclerosis. "It's my own goddamn disease, not some baseball player's." He takes a certain amount of pleasure in rolling the words around on his tongue: amyotrophic lateral sclerosis. He's had it for God knows how long, but it was diagnosed only two years ago when he began dropping things and falling all over the place, and now Dr. Forbes tells him he's got one more year to live, maybe more, maybe less. That's why Father LeBlanc is here, helping out. "Helping out" is a euphemism for doing every goddamn thing there is to do—masses, confessions, sick calls, the corporal and spiritual works of mercy, the whole megillah, you name it—because Father Tom Moriarty is on his last legs. Or rather, off them. This disease, which can strike anywhere, has hit him in the extremities. His feet went first, then his legs, his arms, and his hands. It's working around to his lungs and his heart, he supposes, which is not a bad way to go, considering how his mother went. Father Moriarty had watched, horrified, as she died, and he knows what the disease will do. He also knows it is not hereditary, but a lot of good that does him, since—hereditary or not—he's got it. With his mother, ALS struck the throat muscles first, and she lost her ability to eat and then to talk. In no time at all there she was, walled up inside her body, writing notes until she couldn't hold the pencil anymore, then pushing her finger from letter to letter on a Ouija board, and finally just letting it all happen: a mind ticking over nicely but uselessly, silenced forever by ALS, with no more exercise of intellect or will possible. Just surrender. Just a human being buried alive, but not dead yet. It took a little more than a year before death finished her off.

He, on the other hand, is a lucky bastard. He still has his intellect and his will and—goddamn it all—his voice.

"Roh-oh-oh-oh-se," he wails.

Then he lies there waiting, content that he has done his bit.

†

It is hot today, and it's going to get hotter, so Rose Perez has worn her blue cotton shift and her huaraches. She doesn't feel any cooler, but she figures she must be, and in this old house that's important. The rectory is an impossible building, a two-story white clapboard thing with tiny rooms that hold on to the heat in summer and the cold in winter. Rose walks to work every morning, and it always seems to her as she comes up Church Lane that this could be the house in that movie, *Psycho,* if they just painted it black, but of course this one is smaller. It's separated from the church by a parking lot where the kids play basketball in the fall, and people just drive up here for mass and go away afterward, so nobody seems to notice that it's a real old house that could use some work. On the positive side, it's got a good kitchen that was modernized fifteen years ago, so at least it's easy to keep clean.

Rose is downstairs making Father Moriarty's breakfast, orange juice that he will drink, cornflakes that he'll push around in his mouth, and some lovely wheat toast. He won't touch the toast, but he likes to see it on his plate, so he says. The poor father has this terrible disease, but he doesn't seem to take it seriously. Everything's a joke with him, not a funny joke, either, but sort of a bitter one. She will feed him the cornflakes, as much as he'll take, and when he's done fooling around with the rest of the breakfast, she'll get his glass and his water pitcher ready and she'll go back downstairs and start cleaning the house. Then after a while Father LeBlanc will go in and drag Father Moriarty out of bed so he can sit on the portable toilet. He'll wait outside the room for ten minutes or so and then tap at the door and say, "Father?" and the other one will holler, "Yes, goddamn it," or something like that, and Father LeBlanc will go in and wipe the poor old priest's behind and put him back in bed. Then he'll empty the toilet pan. He insists on doing it himself, Father LeBlanc. He insists on cleaning his own bedroom and his own bathroom. Sometimes he even insists on making his own breakfast. He's quiet and he's unhappy and there's nothing Rose can do about it because he's so distant that it would take a miracle to break through that shell. He would be a handsome, sexy-looking guy if he'd laugh a little. She figures that, even though he's young, he's one of those old-fashioned priests, private and conservative, with a real vocation. Or maybe he's a little touched in the head. After all this time she's still afraid of him. And attracted to him also.

She arranges Father Moriarty's breakfast tray, checks to make sure everything is there, and she adds a bud vase with a single yellow beach rose. It's a thin, fragile-looking thing, starved, with a tuft of dark yellow in the center. She starts upstairs with the tray.

"Roh-oh-se" from above.

Rose pays no attention to Father Moriarty. She is looking at the yellow beach rose and she is thinking of her daughter, Mandy. Mandy is tall and pale, raggedy, but she is tough and defiant and, at sixteen, she is determined to wreck her life. There is nothing Rose can do about it. Rose herself was sixteen when she got pregnant and dropped out of school, and she is hoping Mandy won't repeat her errors. But she probably will. She's boy crazy, and she drinks and she runs around with a fast crowd. She needs a father.

Rose pauses at the head of the stairs and checks the tray once again. Everything is fine. She is still thinking of Mandy as she goes down the corridor, taps at the door, and pushes it open. It is the wrong door, and she is in Father LeBlanc's room. He is kneeling upright at the prie-dieu, his eyes clenched shut, his face twisted somehow, in anger or in pain. "Excuse me," she says quickly and backs out, but Father LeBlanc gives no sign of having heard her enter or leave. *Jesus, Maria,* Rose says to herself, because she feels bad that she never prays and here is this young priest, some kind of saint maybe, in agony. And so good-looking, too. She thinks of her dream last night and wonders if blundering into his room was really a mistake or did she do it deliberately?

Father Moriarty is just about to sing out again when Rose knocks and pushes open his door. "Good morning, Father," she says, deliberately avoiding his glance. She places the little tea rack over his chest, then settles the tray on it, preparing to feed him. "I heard you calling me," she says, "but a person can only move so fast, if you know what I mean. And bread doesn't toast any quicker by yelling at it. You know? So that's why you shouldn't be yelling at me all morning while Father LeBlanc is trying to do his prayers, excetera." She leans forward with a spoon. "Open up."

Father Moriarty listens to her and lets himself be fed.

"It's gonna be a scorcher today. It's a scorcher already."

"Mm," he says.

"Father LeBlanc is over there in his cassock and Roman collar. He's praying. In this heat. I think he must be a glutton for punishment. Or else a saint. Sometimes I think he must be a saint."

Father Moriarty laughs quietly at this.

"Well, he might be. He could be. He's scary enough to be, if you get me." She waits while he rests a little. "Are you okay? Are you doing okay?"

"It's *et* cetera, not *ex* cetera."

"Don't correct me. It's rude to correct people."

He winks at her and says, "*Et,* with a *t.*"

"Drink this juice, it's good for you."

He won't touch the toast and he's eaten very little of the cornflakes, but he's exhausted now, so Rose removes the tray and puts it on the bureau and then folds up the little tea rack. She fills the pitcher with water and places it, with a clean glass, on his night table.

"All right?" she says. "All set? Mrs. Schwartz will be in just after lunch to give you your bath."

Father Moriarty smiles and leans his head forward.

Rose sits on the side of the bed and bends over him until their foreheads touch. They rest this way, her brow against his. There is nothing sexual about this, nothing sensual even, just a solid presence of one to the other. This is a ritual between them.

The first time it happened, it was almost by accident. She had just discovered that her daughter was drinking and perhaps even taking drugs, and sick with worry, Rose suddenly felt she could not go on for one more minute, and she lowered her head until her brow rested against Father Moriarty's. Just for a moment. Just for a couple seconds. And then she sat up and said she was sorry. "No," he said, "that's very good." He said, "Thank you." And, unembarrassed, uncomprehending, they have done this ever since.

"I'll tell Father LeBlanc you're ready," she says. "I'll knock on his door."

†

Father LeBlanc keeps a rigorous schedule. He gets up at five-thirty each morning, runs from five-forty-five to six-forty-five, showers, prays from seven to eight, helps Father Moriarty from eight to eight-forty-five, says nine o'clock mass, makes his breakfast, and then the day begins.

This morning has been like all the others since he has come to Our Lady of Victories. He got up, groggy, headachy, and stumbled to the bathroom. He had an erection, which he ignored—as he always ignores anything to do with the body—and he peed and washed his face and got into his running clothes while he was still half conscious. He put on running shoes and gym shorts and a T-shirt. Everything he wears is faded, dirty-looking, and he prefers that because in school and even in the seminary he was told too often how good he looked. He is not interested in looking good; looks are a snare and a delusion. So he runs early in the morning, before anybody else is around.

He lets himself out of the parish house quietly, just in case Father Moriarty is still sleeping, and he walks past the church and the parking lot and then he begins to jog.

He jogs down Church Lane to the beach road, increasing his pace as he goes. He moves quickly past the two-story Bide-a-Wee apartments and the Tastee-Freeze and the long line of private cottages, and when he gets to Carberry's General Store, with its single gas pump and its tiny post office, he turns left onto the access path to the beach. There is eel grass growing alongside the path, and some kind of pinkish flower with gray leaves, and ahead of him stretches out the endless expanse of green and blue water. At once he is struck by the wet breeze and the dank smell of the receding tide. He runs full-out on the hard wet sand, his pounding heels sending little shocks up through his whole body, until he gets that pain in his chest, and then, instead of slowing down, he sprints. He hears the waves and the gravelly undertow, he sees the gulls swooping and the silly sandpipers, and he knows the salt air must be stinging his face and his eyes, but he feels nothing except the heat spreading in his chest. His mind goes numb and the pain fills him up and he sprints. He would go on—he wills himself to go on—until he dies or explodes or implodes or whatever happens to you when the heart gets too big for your chest, but finally his body gives out, it simply refuses to go on, and he slows, despite himself, to a stumbling run and then a jog and then a hard walk. He stops finally and stands bent over, facing the water, his hands clutching his shins, and he tries not to throw up. Then he starts to move again, walking slowly, walking faster, jogging, and he continues jogging for the full hour. He does not die this time nor any time.

He jogs back up Church Lane and goes inside. He showers, dresses in his black pants and T-shirt, puts on his cassock and his

Roman collar, and he kneels, anguished, and prays. Every day he does this, and it never gets easier.

Now, summoned by Rose's knock on the door, he finishes his prayer, makes the sign of the cross, and gets ready to take care of Father Moriarty. This is the hardest part of the day.

†

Rose puts the breakfast tray on the kitchen counter and begins to tidy up. She rinses the dishes and puts them in the washer. She sponges down the counter. She takes a handful of paper towels and puts a shine on the toaster, the microwave, the stovetop, the faucets. She is quick and thorough. A wet sponge mop to the kitchen floor and, while she's at it, the floor of the guest bathroom as well. The only guest they ever have is Monsignor Glynn, who comes up once a month to visit Father Moriarty, but it's part of the rectory and she cleans it every day.

Rose tries to say a Hail Mary as she works, but she gets only as far as "Blessed art thou amongst women" and her mind is off to some other thing, to Mandy usually. Rose is thirty-two and still good-looking, or at least sexy-looking, but Mandy is the only thing in life that matters to her. Rose has a drink now and then, and sometimes—not very often, but when the loneliness gets bad and she can't help herself—she goes down to Salisbury Beach and lets herself get picked up and she screws the night away. The next day she goes to confession and resolves to do her penance, amend her life, and sin no more, ever again. And God knows, that's what she wants, but sometimes the hollow in her groin hurts so bad she doesn't even want to think about it. And she doesn't think about it. She just acts upon it, she does anything they want to do, and she does it all without thinking. Later she will hate herself for her weakness, but then she goes to confession—in Cobb Point, a different parish—and starts all over again. She is a sinner, she knows that, and she will probably go on sinning for the rest of her life, but she prays to the Virgin Mary over and over, and she believes—a secret belief that has nothing to do with faith—that in the end the Virgin will save her. Deep down she suspects the Virgin Mary doesn't take sex as seriously as the priests do.

She scrubs the toilet bowl and rinses out the brush. When she first came to work at the rectory, she was embarrassed by the idea of being in a house where priests slept and ate and used the toilet. But now the rectory is just like any other old house at the beach, except the bathrooms are new and the kitchen is modern, and priests are like everybody else, only a little neater. It's an easy house to keep clean. She sponges everything in the bathroom; she runs paper towels over all the surfaces until the tile and the chrome gleam. Her toilet at home is a joke. It's got a hairline crack in the bowl, so there's always a tiny puddle of rusty water around the base. Very attractive. And Mandy would rather die than mop it up. But of course the whole apartment is a joke. It was never intended to be an apartment. It was just a big storage attic over a boat repair and clam shop right on the water until Sal, who owned the Clam Box, moved in and fixed it up. That happened because Sal's wife found out he was fooling around and kicked him out of the house. He tried to move in with the girlfriend, but she wouldn't have him either so he took over the storage attic, installed a toilet and a refrigerator, and called it home. Eventually Sal put in a stove and a closet, and he walled off the back part and made it a bedroom. He got a new girlfriend. She wasn't sure about moving in, but she was sure that if she did, she would want a bathtub. He put in a bathtub, he put in a sink with a cabinet, he walled off a tiny room as a bedroom for her baby daughter. But then his whole life changed: his girlfriend found somebody else, and his wife took him back. The attic apartment stood empty until Rose showed up with her ten-year-old daughter. Sal let her stay there free in return for filling in at the Clam Box. But he wasn't interested in making repairs; he made that clear from the start. Rose has lived here now for six years, and everything is falling apart, and the place is definitely a joke. But what can you do?

She hears Father Moriarty's toilet flush and she glances up at the ceiling. There's not much that's private in this house. Father LeBlanc will be coming down any minute to go over to the church and say mass. She would go to mass herself if she were a better woman, but she's not.

She dusts the four small rooms downstairs—the dining room, the guest bedroom, the visitor's parlor, the office—and she runs the vacuum over the carpets, and then she's nearly done.

She'll make some kind of lunch now for Father Moriarty and leave it in the fridge for Father LeBlanc to give him. Mrs. Schwartz, the home-help lady, will come after lunch to bathe him and change the sheets and cheer him up, all of which he hates, so Rose sometimes comes back in the late afternoon for a little visit. They have a chat, which is nice, and Father LeBlanc is never there because he's visiting at the hospital or the prison or somewhere, spreading his idea of good cheer. Poor Father LeBlanc. She dreamed about him last night—a sex dream—and it comes to mind once again, but she pushes it away. "Hail Mary, full of grace. The Lord is with thee. Blessed art thou amongst women." Nonetheless, she sees his naked chest as it was in the dream, and she puts her tongue to it, teasing, but then— thank God—the phone rings and she runs to answer it.

"Our Lady of Victories," she says into the phone, happy again.

†

Father Moriarty lies in bed with his eyes closed. He is recovering from the exhaustion of being taken out of bed, put on the toilet chair, and given five minutes to evacuate his bowels. He's done it, too. And then having Father LeBlanc scrub away at his bum, the sour smell of shit poisoning the air, the toilet paper unmanageable, the humiliation perfectly tuned to the Moriarty need for humility—oh yes, he knows he's a spiritual mess—and to Father LeBlanc's desire for self-sacrifice. LeBlanc practically turns inside out with embarrassment and disgust, though he'd die before he'd admit it, busy as he is doing God's work with toilet paper.

The body is a wonderful thing, cha cha cha. And God has his merits, too, more or less.

†

Rose says again, "Our Lady of Victories. Hello?" but there is no response. "Who is this?" she says as her happiness floats away. "Is anybody there?" She hears the sound of breathing, but maybe it is only her own. "What?" she says. She listens once more, and does she hear a moaning sound? "Do you need help?" she asks. "Do you need a priest? The priest is occupied right now. Hello?" But she hears nothing at all, not moaning, not the sound of her own breathing. It's not a serious call. It's not anything. She listens again and then, reluctantly, she hangs up.

Something terrible is happening, she is sure. She has a vision of Mandy lying on the floor, struggling for breath, unable to say "Help me" into the telephone. Is it booze? Is it drugs? Rose stands by the telephone, looking at it, waiting for it to ring again. "Holy Mary," she says, "please help me."

She should phone Mandy and make sure she is all right. But she only stands there, waiting for something to happen.

†

Father LeBlanc has finished his duties with Father Moriarty and he has twenty minutes free before he will celebrate mass. He paces up and down his room, a large attic room with almost no furniture: a bed, a desk, a chair, a kneeler, a bookcase filled with paperbacks on Church history and Scripture and Greek and Latin classics. Two dormer windows look out over the parking lot to the church. The truth is he can't bear it, this house, this heat, this bleak, uninhabitable life. He is drying up inside, turning to stone, and he hates himself, he wants to die, he wants to *do* something, he wants to *mean* something, he wants—what does he want?—he wants to love God, that's why he became a priest in the first place. He wants to love Jesus, but he doesn't seem able to, he doesn't seem able to pray or to give himself or to—what? All his thoughts end in a question. There is no air here. He cannot breathe. He leans against the window frame with his forehead on the glass, and he thinks he is saying, "I want to love you, I want to love you, help me to love you," but he has this swelling in his chest and in his throat and in his brain and he cannot think, and when the pain passes, he finds he is not saying, "I want to love you." He is saying, "I want you to love me." He is shocked and embarrassed. "I want you to love me," he says again, thinking about it now, not just saying it. It is monstrous, outrageous. It is arrogance like Job's to speak to God this way, as if you had some rights, as if you could make demands on him. "I want you to love me," he says again, and means it. Yes, I have rights, too, he thinks.

"I want you to love me," he says aloud, and closes his eyes. For a while everything stops, everything is silent. Then he hears a sound like rain falling. He feels cool even in his cassock and collar. He could kneel here forever, loving, being loved, without tension or anxiety or guilt.

He is free and he thinks he knows what he is saying and he offers it willingly as he lowers his head to his hands.

"Anything," he says. "Anything."

He feels a contraction of his heart, as if a hand has closed about it, gently, but he says it again.

"Whatever you want, no matter how horrible. And I won't ask anything in return."

He wants whatever God wants.

He gets up slowly, makes the sign of the cross, and starts to leave the room. But before he reaches the door, that hand around his heart closes hard, and he thinks, I've done it now, now I'm in for it. He stops, terrified.

His God is a ruthless God with whom you don't make bargains unless you intend to keep them. He is the God of irony. He is the God of terrible, terrifying jokes. And the bargain has been struck, it's done, he's done for.

But isn't this what he's always wanted, to disappear into God? And now it's going to happen. Somehow. He will simply cease to be. He stands by the door, terrified, immobile, and suddenly a cool flush of blood passes through him, from his heart out to his arms, then all over. Like a cool shower. And he smiles—despite his terror—because he is asking nothing for himself except love, and he is ready for anything, and what does he have to lose? Except himself. He is joyful again.

†

Father Moriarty hears Father LeBlanc on the stairs and thinks, Pick up your feet! Why does he insist on trudging through life like a country bumpkin? Huck Finn in clerics. Saint Clodhopper, Saint Shitkicker. Pick up your goddamn feet!

It's the American thing, stomp your way through life, and Father LeBlanc is nothing if not American. Father Moriarty is American, too, of course, but he has a family—or at least he had one—and he thinks about them often and prays for them and remembers his drinking father and his long-suffering, funny mother and his brother, Michael, and his sister, Cathleen. He remembers going to parochial school and dancing with Ellie McNamara and playing baseball, though not well enough to get a college scholarship. Just well enough to get ALS, ha! He comes from Malden, St. Joe's parish, and he is afraid of too many things, and he doubts the existence of God. In this, he supposes, he is not typically American.

Father LeBlanc is typically American. He doesn't come from anyplace at all; he has no background, no roots, no parish. He doesn't even have a family, or at least he's never mentioned one. He sings in the corridor sometimes—show tunes, popular songs—and he has a terrible singing voice. He can't get through ten notes without flatting at least one. He has no problem with being a priest, he has no problem with parishioners, and, most extraordinary, he has no problems with any article of faith. He does not doubt or question the big unshakable doctrines—the incarnation, the resurrection, the redemption—let alone the hokey ones, like papal infallibility. And yet he's been exiled up here because he was a wild priest. Hard to believe, unless, since coming here, he's completely reformed. Or put his brain on hold. What in hell is going on with this boy!

Father Moriarty closes his eyes and thinks, Have mercy on me. Why can't I be nice? Why can't I be humble?

Why can't pigs fly?

†

Father LeBlanc would like to take the stairs in three leaps—he feels that good—but he is always aware of poor Father Moriarty, so he goes down quietly, though he can't help putting a little bounce in his step. He feels great, and he just wants to keep on feeling whatever it was that happened to him in meditation just now—secret abandon, complete surrender. This is true freedom. He wants to celebrate. He starts to sing "Put on a Happy Face" but stops at once because of poor Father Moriarty.

He passes through the entryway and says good morning to Rose, who is standing by the phone lost in thought, and he goes out the front door, ready for anything. But my God, the heat!

A woman is standing there at the foot of the steps, staring up at him. She is wearing a white dress and a big white hat and sunglasses. She looks cool despite the sweltering heat. A tourist. He gives her a big smile.

She steps back, away from him, and shakes her head no, as if she has made some decision, and goes quickly down the walk. She gets into her car, a little Mustang, dark green, and drives away in the direction of town.

He should have asked her what she wanted. He's failed again, but right now he is too full of joy to dwell on it.

"All things cooperate unto good for those who love God," he says to the empty air, and even though St. Paul said it first, it's true. He whistles softly as he crosses the gravel parking lot to the church.

†

Rose dials her own telephone number, but she gets a busy signal. She listens to the angry buzz until it seems to get louder, angrier, and then she puts the receiver back in the cradle.

She goes to the kitchen and makes lunch for Father Moriarty, even though she knows he'll only push it around the plate. A nice tuna salad on a bed of lettuce, with wedges of tomato all around one side. It looks very tempting, very nice. She covers it with plastic wrap and puts it in the fridge. She should make some iced tea now, but first she will call home and make sure Mandy is all right.

Again, a busy signal.

She slams the phone down. She's getting crazy and there's no need for it. Mandy is probably talking to that new boyfriend, that Jake, with his shaved head and the gold ring in his nostril. He looks like a doper; he looks like a rapist, frankly. She rushes to the bathroom, thinking she will throw up, but nothing happens. It's just nerves. And there's no need for it, there isn't, there really isn't. It's true that Mandy took an overdose once—they never did find out what the drug was—and had to be rushed to the hospital to have her stomach pumped, but that was a long time ago when she was hanging with a bad crowd. She's beyond all that now. At sixteen, she has straightened out. She's going to be all right. She's a good girl.

The phone rings. Rose snatches it up and says hello. There is silence on the line.

"Our Lady of Victories," she says. "Hello?"

A man's voice, muddy-sounding: "Mandy is sick. You'd better get home and take care of her."

"Who is this?" she says. "What do you mean, she's sick?" She listens, but there is only silence. Into the silence, she says, "Jake?" No answer.

She leaves the house at once, hurrying down the front walk. Then she goes back to check; yes, she has put the tuna salad in the refrigerator for Father Moriarty's lunch. He will have Ensure for his dinner. Everything is all set. She locks the front door and starts out at a good pace.

Her apartment over the Clam Box is in the center of town. It's a twenty-minute walk, but walking is quicker than calling a cab because you can never depend on cabs in this town. They come or not depending on how they feel down there. For a second she wishes she had gotten her car out of the shop. It's a junker, really—Father Moriarty gave it to her when it was clear he wouldn't be driving anymore—but it's been at Don's Auto Body for over a month. Don had to order parts and she told him to take his time. The truth is, she doesn't want Mandy driving. Mandy is in enough danger just living. Rose increases her pace and decides that as soon as she hits the beach road, she'll hail a ride from somebody. The thing is to get there as quickly as possible.

"My daughter is sick," she says aloud. "She may be dying."

She reaches the beach road and walks a little faster. The heat is not important. Getting there is important.

But this panic is ridiculous, when she thinks about it. Mandy was lying in bed lazy as a cat this morning when Rose left for work, and she's only been gone a couple hours. How much could happen in a couple hours? There is no need for all this worry. She slows down a little. Mandy is perfectly fine, probably.

She thinks of Jake and that ring in his nostril and she walks a little faster. There are no cars on the road yet; the tourists are still in bed and the locals are at work. A delivery truck pulls alongside her and the driver honks his horn. She tries to wave him down, but he only waves back, blowing a kiss, and then he shoots on ahead. She keeps on walking.

"Hail Mary, full of grace, the Lord is with thee." She will say Hail Marys all the way home and then everything will be all right and she'll get there before anything bad can happen. She makes this promise to the Virgin Mary: If everything is okay at home, I will go to mass every morning for a week. For two weeks or a month. She'll reform her life and she'll be good and she'll stop nagging Mandy to stay in school and study and become somebody. Though maybe she should be nagging Mandy, maybe that's her duty as a mother. Or maybe not. She'll talk to Father Moriarty about it.

She has reached the town, and there are cars here and there, but she's only a couple minutes from home, so a ride wouldn't be any help now. She passes Carberry's and the gas pump on the right, but she crosses to the beach side so she won't have to talk to anybody who might stop for gas. She just wants to get home to Mandy. Her heart is going very fast now.

A car slows down and somebody shouts hello. It's Nick Pappas, who owns the hardware shop. He flirts with her, and he's very sexy, even though he's a good fifty-five. Once last June, over a year ago now, she had sex with Nick Pappas, a onetime thing, a mistake, and she doesn't want to think about it, especially not now. She waves at him and keeps walking, fast.

And then she is home.

†

Father LeBlanc bends low over the altar and whispers the words of consecration. "This is my body," he says. He genuflects, elevates the host, and genuflects again. He prays silently for a moment. "This is my blood," he says. And he thinks, Anything. Whatever you want, I'll give it. But love me.

†

Father Moriarty should be reading his breviary or saying a rosary or meditating on the life of Christ, but he's not doing anything useful like that. He's lying in bed with a sheet over him, existing. He is wondering what all this means: to be born and live for a while and then die. As he sees it, there's nothing profound about this; it's just a puzzle. Some people have nice lives and some people get shit. And what difference does it make, he wonders, except to them. The good live and die. And so do the bad. And the smart and the ignorant. And the rich and the poor. And then some—they must be special ones, they must be selected from the beginning of eternity—some people are born into suffering and abuse and contempt and never know what it is to laugh or to hope or to love somebody. And some, like himself, have it all. They get everything: a nice family, good schools, endless choices, and then—bang, here I come, ready or not— a vocation to the priesthood and no suffering at all. Just a friendship at best, and then, in time, some loneliness, and finally, at the end, despair. Meanwhile, of course, there's a whole bunch of baptisms and weddings and funerals and, just to get your attention, a dash of amyotrophic lateral sclerosis. Then you crumple up a little, shrivel a little, and the next thing you notice is that you're in a position where all you can do is think. You can't walk or eat or even shit without help from somebody else, and even the slowest intellect comes to realize that God is telling you something about the nature of life and death. If there is a God.

†

Rose goes up the outside stairs to her apartment above the Clam Box. The door is unlocked, it stands slightly ajar. Slowly she pushes it open. "Hello," she calls, and again, "hello?" She goes inside and shuts the door. She moves through the kitchen into the living room. "Mandy?" There is only silence. She looks around the room and it's a mess, but it's the same mess she left this morning. She looks into her bedroom, the hall closet, the bathroom. Her heart is beating very fast. And then, not wanting to, she shoves open the door to the bedroom and looks inside.

Mandy is lying facedown, her nightgown rucked up to her waist, one arm hanging off the bed. The phone, with the receiver off the hook, is on the floor, just out of reach. She is deathly white.

Rose crouches beside her, feeling for a pulse. She listens for the sound of breathing, but she hears only her own heart, pounding. "Mandy, sweetheart," she says softly, "are you all right? You're gonna be all right, don't worry. It's all right, sweetheart." She listens for Mandy's heartbeat, and her own heart is beating very fast. She eases Mandy over on her side, and then she sees that blood running from her nose has crusted on her lips and there is white stuff, vomit, hardening on her chest. So it is drugs after all. Rose looks around for any sign of what she's taken: an empty bottle, a nickel bag, anything.

She can't seem to focus. She should be calling someone for help. The doctor, the police. There is a sound from the bed, half choke, half gasp, and then there is a long silence.

Rose puts the phone back on the hook and thinks. Instead of 911 she dials the number for Dr. Forbes, just in case he's home. And awake. And sober. The phone rings and rings. She is about to hang up when old Forbes answers. "Ayuh," he says, "ayuh," he will be glad to come, and he will come right away because drugs are a terrible thing. And she should stay calm in the meanwhile. She should take a good shot of bourbon. Or make herself a cup of tea. Whichever she prefers.

Rose gets a washcloth and cleans the hardened blood from Mandy's nose and lips. She feels her forehead. And once more she feels for a pulse. Then she kneels by the bed and places her hand on Mandy's heart. It's too late this time, she knows it, but she won't accept it. "Please," she whispers, "please don't take her." The tears start, but she brushes them away and says, with anger in her voice, "I'm asking you, please!" And at once she realizes she must get the priest, Father LeBlanc will help, he'll be able to do something. He'll be able to keep Mandy from dying. He's a holy man and he's always praying and he'll know what to do.

Still on her knees, she dials the number for the rectory, but she gets the answering machine. Of course. Father LeBlanc is still in church, saying his prayers after mass. She hangs up, but then at once she picks up the receiver and dials again. He'll have to come back to eat something. Or to look in on Father Moriarty. He's got to. She waits for the message to end, and then she says, "It's me, Rose. Please come right away, please. It's Mandy." She gets up then, and with only a glance at Mandy's body lying there motionless, she leaves the apartment and runs down the stairs to the Clam Box. Sal is behind the counter, setting up for the day, and he nods to her as she comes in.

"Sal," she says, "you've gotta help me," but then she stops because she spots Jake, with the ring in his nostril, nodding over a cup of coffee. She goes to him and sees at once that he is on something, some kind of drug.

"What did you give her? What did she take?"

Jake raises his head and looks at her and frowns.

She yanks that stupid knitted cap off his shaved head. "Listen to me, you little shit," she says. "What did you give her?"

"Hey, man," he says, "that's my hat."

"Was it cocaine? Was it heroin? What was it?" She shakes him by the shoulder, hard.

Jake looks at her as if she has just come into focus. "She had some pills, man, and a little coke, and I went to the bathroom to take a leak, and when I came back she already took the rest of the coke and I barely had a sniff, and then she like freaked. That's it, man. Sayonara. So I got her over to the bed so she could sleep it off."

"Go get the priest."

"She'll be okay."

"Go get the priest, I said."

"She'll sleep it off. Don't have a conniption fit."

"Hey, shit-for-brains," Sal says from behind the counter, "do what she says. Hear?"

Rose digs her fingers into Jake's shoulder. "I'm telling you what to do. I'm telling you go get the priest, Father LeBlanc, up at the church. He'll be finished mass by now. Get him and bring him back here."

Carefully Jake starts to get up from the table.

"Now!" She slaps him with his knitted cap and shoves him toward the door. She follows him and waits until he gets on his motorcycle and takes off in the direction of the church.

Sal comes out of the clam shop.

"Trouble, huh," he says.

Rose is watching Jake out of sight.

"You okay?" Sal says.

"I swear to God, I swear I'll kill him."

"Hey, Rose," Sal says, and puts his hand on her arm.

Rose pulls away, tosses Jake's knitted cap in a trash can, and hurries up the stairs to the apartment.

†

Father LeBlanc is kneeling in the sacristy, making his thanksgiving after mass, but now he feels nothing, not love, not longing, not anything. His brain has been scraped clean. He can't even think, let alone feel.

"Ask anything," he whispers, but he realizes he doesn't mean it now. It was a moment of craziness, this offer. Is it too late to take it back?

†

Rose kneels beside the bed, her fingers on Mandy's wrist. She can feel no pulse at all. She places her fingers on that big vein in Mandy's neck but she feels no pulse there either.

"Oh God," she cries, and she lays her cheek against Mandy's.

Sal has come up the stairs behind her and stands at the bedroom door watching. He crosses the room now and puts his hand

46

on Rose's shoulder. She collapses back on her heels, her head buried in the sheets.

Sal looks at Mandy lying there. He has served in the Korean War, and he has seen a lot of dead bodies, and he sees death on the face of this one. What in hell is he supposed to do?

"Rose," he says. He bends over and feels Mandy's wrist, but it's as he thought. There isn't any pulse. Gently, he closes her eyes. And, just to be sure, he tries once more for a pulse.

"Rose," he says, but he can't bring himself to tell her. Instead he says, "We should call the doctor."

Rose nods, silent.

"I'll call him," Sal says. "I'll call Forbes."

"I've called him," Rose says, her voice muffled. "He's coming."

"Oh." Sal moves to the window overlooking the parking lot and stands there with his back to it, facing the bed. "I'll just wait, then," he says.

†

Father LeBlanc is embarrassed by this whole thing: the ecstatic prayer, the melodrama, asking to be loved. Get a grip, he tells himself. He makes the sign of the cross and pushes himself up from the kneeler.

He is startled to discover that doper, Jake Faria, standing at the door of the sacristy, watching him.

"Jeez," he says, "did you ever hear of knocking?"

"Rose wants you to come," Jake says. "She told me to tell you."

Father LeBlanc looks at him and sees that he's on some drug or other. Jake works part-time at the Veterans Hospital, and some days he's a walking pharmacy.

"Got it," Father LeBlanc says. He leaves the sacristy, genuflects toward the altar, and starts back to the parish house.

Jake follows him, and as Father LeBlanc disappears inside the kitchen door, Jake hollers, "She's not there."

Father LeBlanc reappears at the door.

"She's not there," Jake says again.

"Where is she? What's the matter?"

Jake shrugs. "Man," he says.

"What's going on, Jake?"

"Oh man, this shit is really bad. This is not good, man."

"Is it Rose or is it her daughter?" Father LeBlanc comes down the stairs and looks hard at Jake. He would like to punch him out good. That stupid nose ring and the shaved head and the snotty look. "Is it something about Mandy?"

Jake shifts from foot to foot.

"Drugs? Did you give her drugs?"

Nothing.

"Too much? An overdose?"

Still nothing.

"Did you call a doctor?"

"Rose sent me to get you."

Father LeBlanc stares into his eyes, but Jake looks away. He puts his fist under Jake's chin and tilts his head up. "You're a piece of shit, Jake, you know that?"

"I know it," Jake says, still not looking.

"A piece of dog shit."

"I know."

"Jesus," Father LeBlanc says, and runs up the stairs to get his car keys.

Jake continues to stand there looking at his feet.

†

Father Moriarty knows something is the matter, but he doesn't know what.

"It's Rose," Father LeBlanc says, "it's something about Rose. Or her daughter. I don't know. But I'll get back here as soon as I can. Do you need anything before I go?"

"What about Rose?"

"I'll be back as soon as I can."

"Where are you going?"

But Father LeBlanc is already thundering down the stairs and out the back door. In a moment Father Moriarty hears the sound of the car starting. And then, a while later, he hears a motorcycle tear across the gravel. Then everything is quiet.

Father Moriarty closes his eyes and thinks of Rose. On the underside of his lids he sees a pool of dark green and he gazes into it, letting his mind go blank, not really praying but hoping. Hoping for Rose. And reflected in the pool he sees Rose crouched on her heels, kneeling, her face buried in a sheet. The sheet covers a small body, dead.

"Oh no," Father Moriarty says aloud, and then he starts to pray.

But to whom can I pray?

He goes on praying anyway.

†

Dr. Forbes has arrived, and he smells only a little bit from alcohol. Rose meets him at the top of the stairs. "It's drugs, I think," she says, her face grim, and leads him into the bedroom where Sal is still standing with his back to the window.

"Well now," Dr. Forbes says, "let's see what we can do here. How are you, Rose, yourself? You're looking fine, very fine. Hello, Sal, you're here, too. Now, let's see what we can do to help this little lady."

Sal gets him a kitchen chair and Dr. Forbes pulls it up to the side of the bed. "Yes, yes," he says, "well, this is not good. No." He places his palm on Mandy's forehead, and then he raises her eyelids, her right and then her left, and finally he takes her pulse. He clears his throat and sits back in the chair. He opens his black bag, looks inside, and closes it again.

Rose, standing by the window next to Sal, asks, "Will she be all right? Is she gonna, you know, be all right?"

Dr. Forbes sits looking at Mandy, his hand on her wrist. After a while he folds her hands across her chest. He pulls the sheet up to her waist.

"Doctor?"

"Don't, Rose," Sal says, and he puts his arms around her.

She lets herself be held, but she keeps looking at Dr. Forbes.

"Well," Dr. Forbes says.

For a long time there is silence in the room. They can hear cars passing in the street outside and they can hear the soft swell of the ocean. The tide is out.

"What did she take?" the doctor asks finally.

"I don't know. Her boyfriend gave it to her. Coke, I think."

"Mmm."

"Or heroin, maybe. Shouldn't we get her to the hospital? Couldn't they pump her stomach?"

"No, I don't think so."

"Couldn't they do *something*?"

Dr. Forbes feels again for a pulse, but of course there is nothing.

"Please!"

Dr. Forbes gets up and comes over to Rose and, awkward, Sal releases her from his embrace. Dr. Forbes takes her hands in his and says, "This is an awful thing, Rose, but you've got to face it. Mandy is dead. She's gone. Whatever she took, she took too much of it. She's dead."

Rose shakes her head, slowly at first and then hard. "No," she says. "She can't be dead. She isn't dead."

Now Dr. Forbes puts his arms around her. "She's gone," he says. "It happened very quick. She was here and then she was gone. I'm deeply grieved for you, Rose, I surely am."

And then Father LeBlanc is here. He crosses the room and, putting aside the chair, kneels by the bed. He takes one of Mandy's hands in his, and though he can see she is dead, he feels for a pulse. He bends over her, his head nearly touching her chest, and prays. Then he takes from his pocket the sacred oils and anoints her lips, her hands, her forehead, saying the required prayers, softly, slowly. It takes a long time.

Rose is kneeling beside him and she waits until he is done.

"She's going to live, though?" Rose asks. "Father?"

"She's passed away, Rose. I'm sorry. I'm so sorry."

"She's dead, you mean? Mandy is dead?"

"Pray with me, Rose. Pray that she will be at peace in heaven with our Lord and our Lady."

"She's not dead," Rose says. "I don't believe it."

"Rose, honey," Sal says. "About these things, this is how it is."

"I'll call the ambulance, Rose," Dr. Forbes says, "and I can declare her—well, deceased, you know—at the hospital, otherwise the police will get involved and there'll be all kinds of investigations going on right here and you'll never get your life back to normal.

I'll take care of everything, my girl. You just say some prayers with Father, here." He moves toward the telephone.

"Get out," Rose says, and when nobody makes a move to leave, she shouts, "get out! I want you out of here, all of you!" And then, as if she has heard how she sounds—like somebody on a television show— she says, "I want to be alone with her. I just want to be alone with my daughter for a minute. Please give me that, please."

Dr. Forbes leaves the room at once and Sal follows him. They stand outside the bedroom door.

Father LeBlanc isn't sure what to do. "I'll pray with you," he says.

"I'm all right," she says to him, "I'm all right now, Father. I just want some time alone with her." He stands there. "Please," she says, "please go."

He goes, closing the door behind him. He hears Rose lock it from the inside.

The three men pass through the living room and the kitchen and stand on the stairs outside the door. The tide is out, and the boats barely rock in the smooth water, and even the gulls are quiet.

"I could use a little something," Dr. Forbes says.

"Poor Rose," Sal says. "She lives for that girl."

"I think I'll be moseying along," Dr. Forbes says. "I'll call that ambulance so she'll die at the hospital officially."

"That's good," Father LeBlanc says.

Dr. Forbes goes down the stairs and gets in his car and drives away. Sal and Father LeBlanc look out over the harbor.

"Poor Rose," Sal says again. He goes downstairs to his clam bar.

†

Rose stands looking at her dead daughter. She can't be dead. She can't be dead. She can't be dead.

"No!" she shouts, "no, no, no," and then she collapses at the foot of the bed, sobbing at last, out of control, violent. She snatches at her hair and pulls it forward over her eyes, she drives her fists into her belly, gouging, she bangs her forehead on the floor. And still she is sobbing.

There is a soft tap at the door, and then another.

"Rose?" It is Father LeBlanc.

She continues sobbing for a long while. Then she gets up and stands near the door. "Yes?" she says.

"I think you should open the door now," he says.

"Yes," she says, "in a little while. I just want to pray alone with her for one more minute."

She goes back to the bed and kneels beside it. She folds her hands in prayer and she closes her eyes and she is determined.

*You've got to be quick,* she says, *you've got to do this right away. The ambulance will be coming and they'll take her and then she'll be dead. I want her back,* she says. *I want her now. Do you hear me?*

†

Dr. Forbes sees that the Lamplighter is just opening its doors, and at once he pulls off the road into the parking lot. Just a quick one, a double Scotch, to get him through the morning. Then he'll call the ambulance. Then he'll get to the hospital. Poor Rose, he thinks, and that poor girl of hers, dead, at . . . what? Fifteen? Sixteen? She's just a child. Drugs are a terrible thing.

He enters the comfortable dark of the cocktail lounge; even empty of customers, it's a welcoming place, with that wonderful morning smell of cigarettes and whiskey. He goes straight to the bar and takes a stool. The bartender is still lugging stuff from the back room, but Dr. Forbes doesn't mind the wait. "Take your time," he says, "don't worry about me," because now his drink is only minutes away. He'll use this time constructively.

He goes to the phone and calls the hospital. An ambulance, he explains. Drugs. Very near death. He'll be there at the hospital to meet the ambulance. Have a good day.

And so he's done his duty and his conscience is clear.

"Dewars," he calls to the bartender, "a double. When you get a chance."

†

Rose is praying to the Virgin Mary. She is pleading. She is insisting.
"Now!"

She is out of her head.

†

Father Moriarty lies in bed listening to the cicadas in the grass. Or are they crickets? What is a cicada anyhow? He is supposed to be praying—and he is, in a way—but the sound of that whirring in the grass and the feeling of dry heat in the room and his complete immobility overwhelm him and he can think only of water. A glass of water. A drink of water.

There is a pitcher of water by his bed, and an empty glass, but his arm muscles are completely atrophied and he can move his hand well enough to say the rosary but not enough to wipe his own bum, so how is he going to reach out for the glass, let alone pour water from the pitcher?

He turns his head on the pillow—he can still do that—and he sees the pitcher is within reach. He smiles and closes his eyes.

The inside of his lids is dark green and then dark blue. The color of water. He sees a pool of water, then a lake, then an ocean, and he gazes into it. He would like to pray, really. It would be nice.

†

Father LeBlanc knocks at the door and calls to her. "Rose," he says, "Rose, you've got to open this door. You've got to come out. The ambulance will be here soon."

Rose prays. She is begging the Virgin Mary. She is making promises. "I will never have sex again as long as she lives. Never." But Mandy lies there, white, and she does not breathe. "Please," Rose cries out, "please!"

Father LeBlanc turns away from the door. He goes outside and waits on the steps. The harbor is unnaturally quiet.

†

Father Moriarty, eyes closed and gazing at the ocean, sees the surface break and a face appear, then a whole head, and thick hair fanning out on the dark water. It is a young girl, laughing carelessly, abandoned. Her face is shining. She is a vision, but she is full of life and she will never die.

He opens his eyes and sees the pitcher of water. He reaches out, and with his hand steady, he pours water into the glass until it is full. He drinks the water straight down in one long draft. He was so dry. He pours more water in the glass until it is half full.

He closes his eyes.

He sees nothing now, but he hears the cicadas whirring in the grass. Hosanna, he thinks. Hosanna in the highest. And though he intends to pray, he falls asleep.

†

Dr. Forbes finishes his second double Scotch and eases off the bar stool. It seems higher than when he got on it. He hears the sound of an ambulance and remembers that he has to go to the hospital to pronounce her dead. Rose Perez. Or her daughter, rather. Mandy. He pops a mint into his mouth and, with a wave to the bartender, goes out to his car. He is blinded by the light but only for a moment. He finds himself humming, some church song or other.

†

Rose hears the ambulance in the distance, and she leans over the body, covering it with her own. There is no more time. There is not one more minute. Not a second. She lets out a shriek, long and terrible, one last desperate cry to the Virgin Mary. And then it is over.

There is silence, followed by a knocking at the door. Rose pulls herself up from Mandy's dead body, and one last time, she lays her head against her daughter's heart. The girl feels warm, alive. Rose straightens up and looks into Mandy's face, lays her hand against her cheek, strokes it with her thumb. There is a flush to that cheek. Mandy doesn't look dead after all. She looks like she did this morning, just taking a catnap before it's time to get up. "Mandy," Rose whispers, and strokes her cheek again. She could swear the girl's lashes moved, but of course that's a trick of the light. Or she herself caused the lashes to move when she touched Mandy on the cheek. The lashes twitch once again and, for a second, Mandy's eyes flutter open.

Rose collapses back into herself. She cannot breathe. She cannot speak.

Another knock at the door.

Mandy's eyelids flutter once again.

Slowly Rose gets up from beside the bed and opens the door. Father LeBlanc comes in, followed by the EMTs, and they go over to the bed. Mandy lies there with her eyes open, trying to focus. Then she frowns and pushes back her hair with one hand.

"What?" Mandy says. "What's the matter?"

They stand and look at her. There is no sound in the room except the alarm clock ticking on the night table.

"I took too much stuff," she says. "I've got a headache." She looks from her mother to the priest to the EMTs, and recognizing them, she says, "Hi, Renny. Hi, Toom."

"Looking good," Renny says.

"Hi," Toom says, and licks his lips in that sexy way he does whenever he sees her. Then he smiles, embarrassed, because the priest is there.

Rose moves away from them, her back to the wall.

"Well, it don't look like you need us," Renny says.

"I need some aspirin," Mandy says. She touches her chest and feels the crusted vomit there. "And a shower."

"Well, if you think we should go," Renny says.

"Go," Rose says, suddenly eager. "Yes, go. She's fine. She's all right." She leads them out through the living room and the kitchen. "I'm sorry to trouble you," she says. "Mandy's sorry too."

"You take care," Renny says. "Care," Toom says, and turns back for a last look at Mandy. They let themselves be pushed out the door.

In the bedroom Father LeBlanc is standing, struck dumb. Rose comes in, brisk and efficient, and says, "Thank you for coming, Father," and tries to move him toward the door. "She's all right now. She'll be all right."

"She was dead," Father LeBlanc says. His voice is thin, incredulous, as if there is no breath behind it. "I saw with my own eyes that she was dead."

"But she's all right now," Rose says. "She was unconscious, that's all."

She sounds matter-of-fact, but she is trembling. She says, "Please, Father," and again she tries to move him toward the door.

"It's a miracle," he says, whispering. "She was dead, I know it. You know it too."

"She was unconscious," Rose says. "Please. You've got to go."

Father LeBlanc does not know what to do. He would like everything to be as it was, but it isn't, and it will never be that way again.

"Thank you, Father," Rose says, and closes the door behind him. She locks it.

She goes down on her knees there in the kitchen, and if she dared to speak, she would say *Thank you, thank you*, to the Virgin Mary. But she says nothing, and she thinks nothing. She is very afraid. She cannot stop shaking.

†

Father Moriarty wakes, thirsty. He has been dreaming, a lovely, cool, reassuring dream about . . . about something, but he cannot remember what. He would like a drink of water. He turns his head on the pillow and sees the pitcher and the glass. The glass, he notices, is half full. If he had any muscular control, he could reach out and pick it up and slug it down. But he has no control, not over his muscles, not over anything. So he will just have to wait.

# THREE

FATHER LEBLANC LEAVES ROSE'S APARTMENT AND drives toward home. He is giddy, he is joyful, he is terrified. "Well, I've never been to a miracle before," he says aloud. He is a lunatic.

The car swerves across the white line, and an oncoming truck honks at him. He waves—sorry—at the driver and laughs because he can't keep from laughing. How are you supposed to react to a miracle? Rose seems to have simply denied it. Dr. Forbes is as confused as always. And Sal?

As for himself, he knows a miracle when he sees one.

His mind races: Rose, Mandy, God's will, God's whimsy, his own little pact with God. Love me and do with me what you will. Is the miracle a sign of something? Acceptance? The vanity of it, the sheer arrogance, strikes him head-on, and he veers off the road onto the sandy shoulder and brings the car to a stop. He's got to get a grip. He's got to talk to someone about what this means.

He could tell Father Moriarty, but Father Moriarty would just laugh. Father Moriarty thinks he's a spiritual moron. Which is true, so how come he gets to witness a miracle? Can it be that God has actually come knocking at his door?

†

Rose Perez stands at the kitchen window and looks out over the quiet harbor. It smells, as always, of low tide and brine and wet wood. And today there is the smell of creosote and the sound of hammering. Early in the morning, the harbor is busy with fishing boats—trawlers, lobster boats, purse seiners with their little tender-boats and their half-moon nets—but in the afternoon, sailboats move quietly out to sea and back again, powerboats and sloops and ketches and cutters. There is even an old wooden schooner moored in the distance; it never goes out, it only rides the dark water.

The water is slate-colored, flat, as the sun disappears momentarily behind a bank of clouds. Gulls swoop above the fishing boats shrieking, on the lookout for fish or fish bait or garbage. They love orange peels. Rose tries to concentrate on gulls and orange peels, but her mind leaps back to what has happened, and once again she leaves the window and goes to the bedroom to check on Mandy.

Mandy is not unconscious, she is just resting; you can tell the difference. Rose has looked in on her every few minutes, and now, an hour later, it is clear there has been no mistake. Mandy is alive. Her forehead is cool, her skin is clear. She shows no effects of a drug overdose. She is merely worn out from the ordeal.

Rose returns to the window and tries to bend her mind around the facts. Mandy was dead, they all knew it. And now, thanks to the Virgin Mary, she is alive.

Rose hears Mandy get out of bed and runs to her. "How are you, Mandy? How are you now?"

"I need a shower," Mandy says, stretching. Then she looks at her mother. "What?" She is ready for a fight but decides to be nice instead. "You all right, Mom?"

"You were dead . . . almost. You almost died."

"I freaked a little. It's not that big of a deal."

Rose feels around for the words. She doesn't know how to ask this: "What was it like when you were out?"

"Out is out, right?" Mandy says. "It was like . . . nothing."

"You don't think you were—dead?"

Mandy laughs, that smart sarcastic laugh all the kids have. "Yeah, right."

"And came back?"

"I've gotta shower," Mandy says, and goes into the bathroom.

†

Dr. Forbes leaves the hospital as soon as he decently can—he feels obliged to say hello to everybody so they can see he's not drunk—and then he heads for home. His sister, who keeps house for him, has a nice lunch on the table. A cold soup, gazpacho, and some lovely French bread. But he's not in the mood to eat.

"You've got to eat something," she says. "You don't eat enough."

He sits down at the table, but at once he gets up and goes to the buffet, where he pours himself a tall Scotch and water. His sister frowns, but he doesn't care. He needs the drink.

"I'm cracking up," he says.

"But slowly," she says.

"I thought a girl was dead today—Rose Perez's daughter—and I was ready to pronounce her dead, but she wasn't. She was only unconscious. Drugs. She woke up, thank God, before I pronounced her dead officially. I'd have looked like a horse's ass."

His sister listens with her head tilted, which indicates she is trying to understand what he really means beneath what he's saying. He's seen her do this often enough.

"I mean, I'm sure there was no pulse."

63

"Maybe she *was* dead."

"Then she woke up and said she had a headache."

"Maybe she was dead and then she came back to life."

Dr. Forbes looks at his sister. She is a maiden lady of nearly seventy. She has never married and she is religious and she is probably suffering from some kind of sexual deprivation. They often turn to religion as a last resort.

"She was not dead," he says. "Period."

"Fine. Then you're cracking up," his sister says.

†

Father Moriarty hears someone on the stairs and recognizes the sounds of Mrs. Schwartz, the home-help lady. She will give him his bath, change his sheets, and rig him out for another lively afternoon and evening in bed. Ta-daa! Poor woman, going from corpse to corpse, washing it, changing it, putting it back to bed. And here she is.

"Ah, Mrs. Schwartz," he says.

"Father," she says, a breakthrough for them, since until recently she has called him nothing at all.

Mrs. Schwartz looks around the room with disapproval. It is a large attic room, but for a sickroom it is small and nasty. Father Moriarty has his toilet chair on the far side of the bed, as it should be for privacy, and a reclining chair next to his bed so she can give him a change of position now and then, but there is clutter everywhere and not enough air, despite the nice dormer windows that look out on a pine grove. A walker he no longer uses has been pushed off to a corner; there is a chest of drawers crowded with all the things needed to wash him and change him and give him his meds. There is a standing lamp by the bed and a table lamp on the nightstand. His books are piled everywhere, and right next to his bed is a fat red paperback called *Documents of Vatican II* and beside it *Anna Karenina,* which she is not sure she approves of, for a priest anyway. His reading glasses, rosary beads, a ChapStick, cough drops, nail clippers, a stray key, a pitcher with water and a water glass: all this on a little table up near his pillow . . . in a room with a roof that slants down one side almost to the floor . . . this is far from being an ideal sickroom.

"Nothing's changed," he says.

"I don't like change," she says. "I do like neatness."

He smiles at her as if he means it, and suddenly he discovers he is very glad to see her. "Mrs. Schwartz," he says. "You're a wonder."

†

Father LeBlanc sees Mrs. Schwartz's car in the parking lot and makes a U-turn straight back to the Clam Box and Rose's apartment.

†

"I'm telling you, she was dead," Sal says, stirring up the coleslaw so that the faded stuff goes to the bottom. He sniffs it. It's okay, just a little discolored. "She was out, gone. I checked her pulse twice, and there was nothing. *Muerto.* Gonno."

Luis, the busboy, nods, and says, *"Sí."*

"Get that table in the corner, Luis, it's got some coffee rings and shit on it. Then put those plates in the steamer and get to work on the new barrel of clams. Okay? And watch out with the shells. Anyhow, she wakes up and says, like, 'I've got a headache.' No shit."

*"Sí,"* Luis says, busy with the table in the corner. All the tables have coffee rings that never come off.

"I'm telling you," Sal says, but he stops as the door opens and Father LeBlanc comes in. "Father," he says. "Close call, eh?"

"Close."

"I thought she bought the farm."

Sal leans across the counter grinning, and suddenly Father LeBlanc notices a kind of lust in his grin, as if this miracle were a superior kind of trick. He wanted confirmation that Mandy was dead, and so he came to Sal, but now he wants only to keep it secret. You have to protect a miracle.

"Well, I guess we were wrong," Father LeBlanc says.

"You think so? I coulda swore she was dead."

"Could I have a coffee, Sal? Black?"

"I was convinced she was dead. You didn't think she was dead?"

"Yeah, sure, but obviously we were wrong. Leaping to conclusions."

Sal pours the coffee just as the door opens and four kids, then another, come in. They're pushing and shoving, horsing around.

"Hey, *hey!*" Sal says, a bark the kids understand. They quiet down for a second and then they start ordering, all at the same time. Sal ignores them and says to Father LeBlanc, "I guess she couldn't've been dead, right? She looked it, though. Drugs, man." He shakes his head. "You know what I mean?"

"I know," Father LeBlanc says.

The kids are horsing around again.

"*Hey!*" Sal hollers, "there's a priest here, y'know!"

Father LeBlanc leaves a dollar for the coffee, and with Sal occupied, he goes out and around the side and up the stairs to Rose's apartment.

†

At the top of the stairs Father LeBlanc stops and looks out over the harbor. There is a cutter out in the distance. Three masts. Its sails just unfurling. The sunlight strikes the sails, making their reflections flicker on the water. He leans on the flaking wood banister and looks. The light shifts and blinds him for a moment. A spark erupts in the corner of his eye. And then another spark. The sparks join to make a flame, and he can only watch what is happening. He is kneeling at his bedroom window, he is praying, then he is running, and the flame pursues him, the flame grows larger, he is encased in fire. Black butterflies descend, beating at his eyes, his mouth, a terrible sound. The smell of burning. And then his vision clears, the fire is out, and he returns to himself.

It was some kind of fit, but now it is over.

For a long time he stands outside Rose's apartment, staring ahead at the purple water.

†

Rose stands at her kitchen window watching the cutter move slowly out of sight. Father LeBlanc, shaken, confused, stands outside her door watching the same cutter move slowly out of sight. Time is suspended for this little minute. Anything is possible. They stand and watch the ship disappear. They are aware of each other, but they keep the door between them. And then he knocks and she opens it.

†

At first Father LeBlanc can find nothing to say. He and Rose Perez are, after all, strangers. They have been brought together by an impossible act: her daughter has risen from the dead. Because of Rose.

Because of her prayers. She is, as he can never be, God's chosen. He steps inside the kitchen, determined at last.

"Somebody has to take control of this situation," he says, too loud. "You know what it is," and then his voice sinks to a whisper. "Rose?"

"Please go," Rose says.

"Look at me." He takes her by the shoulders. "You know it's a . . . miracle." He speaks the word without any breath at all, so that he seems to be moving only his lips.

Rose shakes her head.

"You know it is."

"Please let me alone."

"You should be singing, you should be thanking God, you should be . . . I don't know . . . shouting from the top of the roof." He says this, but he sounds sad, almost angry. "And she should be—I don't know, in a convent or something."

"It's not a miracle."

"She was dead. There's proof. We saw with our own eyes that she was dead. Three of us, no, four of us."

"We made a mistake."

"The *doctor*?"

"He was drinking. He's always drinking."

He pulls her close, their faces almost touching. "It was a miracle," he insists.

She shrinks from him. She is a small animal, cornered. She looks distraught. He wants to take her in his arms and hold her. He wants to inhale her sanctity. He wants to press her body into his own.

For a second he feels a hard tug in his stomach, in his groin, and then, frightened, he leaves.

†

Back at the rectory, he sees Monsignor Glynn's car parked next to Mrs. Schwartz's. Just what he needs. Actually, he could tell Glynn about it—Glynn might even believe it—but there's tension between them about the transfer. It was Glynn who picked this place, Our Lady of Victories, when the bishop wanted to send him to an Indian mission in Arizona. He should be grateful, but still, he has the feeling that Glynn is an enemy. He's on the side of the Church.

In the rectory everything is quiet. There is that smell of waxed floors and cleaning stuff that Rose always leaves behind. As Father LeBlanc lets himself in by the side door, he hears the phone ring and then the machine takes over. He hears his own voice, scratchy and thin, saying, "Please leave a message," a pause, and then a woman's voice, hesitant, saying she will call back later. He doesn't recognize the voice. There is no sign of Glynn. Good. Father LeBlanc goes up the stairs quietly.

"Hey!" Father Moriarty yells. "What's going on?"

Mrs. Schwartz has just finished giving Father Moriarty his bath, and Father LeBlanc uses her as an excuse to avoid telling him anything.

"Everything's all right," he says, leaning into the room. "Hello there, Mrs. Schwartz."

Mrs. Schwartz nods and continues tidying the bedside table.

"So what all happened?" Father Moriarty asks. "What's the damage?"

"False alarm," Father LeBlanc says, "everything's all right."

"I'd like to know, if you don't mind. Come in here."

"Father Moriarty needs a glass of water," he says to Mrs. Schwartz, and without another word, he goes to his room, changes

69

into his jeans and T-shirt, and, bounding down the stairs in his running shoes, leaves the rectory. Monsignor Glynn, coming in from the church, steps aside to avoid a crash with Father LeBlanc. "And hello to you, too," the monsignor says.

Father LeBlanc gets in his car and drives. He heads north. It doesn't matter where he's going; he has no idea, no plans; he is simply driving. He wants out. Anywhere. Canada—he could be driving to Canada. "Why not?" he says aloud, and so he drives north to the Maine border, where he stops for a cheeseburger and Coke. He is trying not to think, but he keeps returning to the blasphemous thought: is this the beginning of sanctity, is this how it goes?

He will be damned, he thinks, for his presumption. This is the worst kind of sin.

He passes a liquor store, but at the next intersection he turns around and goes back. He buys a six-pack of beer. He drives along the coast until he finds a deserted spot off the main road where he can sit looking out over the water, pretending not to think. He is not used to drinking, and by the time he finishes the six-pack, it is night. He is hungry again and a little drunk. He is still sitting by the water and still wondering what this miracle can mean. He tries to pray, but his prayer is absurd. *He* is absurd.

He gets back in his car and drives south toward home. When he sees a beer-and-burgers sign, he pulls over and goes in for a cheeseburger and a draft beer. He has a second beer and is thinking about a third when he realizes he is drunk. He goes into the men's room and tries to throw up. Nothing happens. Outside in the parking lot, he takes a deep breath of the sharp air, gets into his car and closes his eyes to rest for a minute, and, blessedly, falls asleep.

†

Rain begins to fall around midnight, a soft rain at first and then a terrible pelting that sounds like fists beating on the roof. Mandy rolls over in her sleep, sighing, and Rose turns to look at her. Mandy is glowing with youth and good health. Rose herself is exhausted, but of course she cannot sleep. She sits by Mandy's bed for most of the night and then she goes to the living room and sits by the window, watching the rain on the water. She wants to shake Mandy awake, to slap her, to tell her she will not put up with this a minute longer. And then she wants to cradle her in her arms, her baby again, defenseless; she wants to protect her. The world is out there waiting to destroy girls. They think they know everything, they think they will never die, they just want to feel that thing pushing up against them and in them, and they want to go out of themselves. Sex is everything at that age. And booze. And drugs. It's all for freedom, for excitement. If only she could give her own life to protect Mandy's, but she knows she can't, and she knows it will happen again, and she knows there will be no miracle the next time. "Hail Mary," she says aloud, "full of grace," and she thinks she is praying, but maybe she is asleep. It no longer matters. It is all one now.

†

Father Moriarty knows and does not know. He's had a nice visit with Ed Glynn, the love of his life, with his red face and his funny thatch of hair and his great mind. But Ed left at eight, right after the *Barney Miller* rerun, and LeBlanc never showed up to put him on the toilet. So something is up. Huckleberry Finn has a rendezvous with God, no doubt.

Now it is midnight and rain is pelting down in buckets. He sees wooden buckets falling on the house, some with handles, some new and some battered, some leaking water through the loose slats. It is a picture by Magritte and it pleases him. He could press the emergency buzzer that hangs around his neck and connects with the police station, but there is no emergency. The truth is, he feels wonderful. He knows that, for some reason, he is home free now. Whatever that means.

†

Father LeBlanc is walking along the shore in the rain. The sky is a flat gray and the ocean is gray and the rain feels like it will never stop. He looks out to where the horizon should be, but there is only gray sky meeting gray water, without even that thin purple line that tells you where the air ends and drowning begins. He turns and looks down the long row of cottages, dark, every one of them, dark and cold. And the rain is cold.

It is five o'clock in the morning, and for hours now he has been walking by the shore in the rain. His breath is foul and his mouth tastes of stale beer. He has not prayed once all night, unless you count his saying "Oh my God" over and over meaninglessly. He will have to make some sense of this soon.

The girl was dead, not a sign of life, none, and in less than an hour she was living again. He saw it with his own eyes. He walks slowly along the shore in the cold rain.

For a second he wonders: has he imagined all this?

†

"Rose!" Father Moriarty sings out. "Ro-oh-oh-se."

Father Moriarty feels shitty this morning—it's gray out, still pouring rain—so he's trying to compensate by sounding like his old self.

72

"Rose, my darling girl, where are you?" he shouts, and then he listens for a response.

The rain began before midnight and hasn't stopped since. It's almost chilly this morning, perhaps the end of the hot spell. Not that it will make any difference. Hot or cold, you've got to get through it.

And where is that damned LeBlanc?

Father Moriarty hears Rose on the stairs and yells, "Where's my goddamn breakfast!"

She enters smiling and he smiles, too, until he sees her face. She looks ten years older, her eyes are swollen, and her face is very red. He always thinks of her as a pretty girl, but today she looks old, worn out.

"Are you all right?"

"Bread doesn't toast any faster just because——"

"Just because you yell at it, I know. But how are you?"

"I'm fine. I'm just fine." She places the tray on his bureau while she settles the tea rack across his lap. Then she boosts him up with pillows at his back, getting him ready to eat.

"Never mind all that," he says. "I don't want to eat. I want to know what happened. You say you're fine, but you don't look fine."

"I'm all right."

"And Mandy?"

"Mandy is fine."

"Mandy is fine," he says, and the words call back that dream he had, the girl surfacing from beneath the ocean, her thick hair fanning out upon the water, and her face shining. In the dream he reached out and poured himself a glass of water and drank it. But now, as his hands lie nearly helpless at his side, Rose lifts the spoon to his mouth, and as she does their eyes meet.

She puts down the spoon.

"Something happened," she says.

"Yes?"

"Mandy almost died. It was drugs, cocaine probably, and she almost died." She cannot stop herself. "There was no pulse. She had no pulse at all."

"And you prayed."

"And I prayed."

"And then?"

"Then the father came, Father LeBlanc, and he blessed her with the oils and everything."

"Yes?"

"Yes."

Rose cannot bring herself to say it was a miracle. But if she is ever to tell anybody, Father Moriarty is the person she will tell. And now is the best time. Maybe he can show her it was no miracle at all. She listens to the rain beating on the roof.

They hear someone come in the side door and then they hear heavy feet on the stairs. Father LeBlanc, of course. He pauses outside Father Moriarty's door and looks in.

"Good God!" Father Moriarty says.

Father LeBlanc is soaked through, but that is not the worst of it. He needs a shave, he has dark circles under his eyes, and his face looks haggard, hollowed out. His clothes cling to his body.

"Have you told Father?" Father LeBlanc asks Rose.

"I told him Mandy's all right."

Father LeBlanc shivers involuntarily. "Tell him, why don't you," he says, and then he disappears.

"So what is all this about?" Father Moriarty asks.

"He thinks it was a miracle," Rose says.

Father Moriarty makes a snorting sound, not a laugh and not quite a dismissal.

"That's what he thinks," Rose says.

Father Moriarty stares at her, that ravaged face, that closed-off look. "And what do you think?" he asks.

"I didn't graduate from high school. I don't know anything about such things."

"You know the difference between dead and alive." He fixes her with his stare. "Don't you."

She lowers her eyes, her face crimson.

"I've got to feed you and then I've got to go to mass. In thanksgiving. I promised the Virgin. So please be quiet and eat."

And for the first time in a long time, he eats almost all his breakfast.

†

Sal puts the hot dogs on the grill and the buns in the warmer.

"Miracles don't happen anymore," he says to Luis. "Miracles are from the old days with monks and the Dark Ages and, like, Saint Bernadette. But I'll tell you, Luis, she sure as shit looked dead to me."

Luis nods and goes on with his work.

†

Mandy wakes to the sound of the rain letting up. It's cozy to be in bed, with the room just chilly enough so that you need a blanket, and outside it's raining nice and soft. She puts her hand between her legs and imagines it is Jake. "Jake, oh," she says, and then, "oh, oh, oh," but it's not as good as the real thing, so she stops and listens to the rain. She had too much coke, and she freaked, and then the whole world was in her bedroom: her mother and the priest and Dr. Forbes and Sal from downstairs and those cute ambulance guys, Renny and Toom—they're sexy, Toom especially, they know she's hot—and what else? Then she came out of it. With a headache. She remembers the headache. But what she remembers best is the nice sleep she had afterward, a long, long sleep.

And then suddenly it comes to her: her mother asking if she thought she had been dead and came back to life. She shivers and pulls the blankets tight around her. What's the matter with her, anyway, what kind of mother is she? Does she *want* her dead? That's what they'd say in English class, they'd say it's a psychological thing; she asked if you were dead because really she wants you to be. She thinks for a while and decides that maybe that's true in books, but it's not true about her mother. For all her mother's faults, Mandy knows, she only wants her to straighten up and fly right.

She thinks about drugs and she thinks about her mother screaming and carrying on and suddenly she is inspired. No more drugs for the rest of the summer. To please her mom. To make her feel really good for once.

It's nice to be generous.

†

Father LeBlanc is saying mass, and Rose, coming in late, kneels off to the side where she can see but can't really be seen, unless you're looking for her. She is keeping her promise to the Virgin. From where she sits, she can see Father LeBlanc in profile. He has just shaved and showered and his hair is slicked back. There are dark smudges under his eyes from not sleeping. He looks very handsome, very sexy. Rose makes the sign of the cross and asks for forgiveness.

She is the victim of a miracle. She has obligations now to her daughter and to this priest—because, really, it happened through him—but she doesn't know what those obligations are. The best she can hope for is that Mandy will stay off drugs for a while, maybe for good. And then there is the priest. What does she owe the priest? Well, she thinks, she can start by not having dirty thoughts about him, that's for sure, that's one thing.

†

Father LeBlanc has noticed the woman in the hat, and already distracted by the miracle, he gives way to another distraction and allows himself to wonder where he has seen her before. She is young and, he supposes, beautiful. And troubled. At once he remembers that she came to the rectory yesterday morning—yesterday, which seems a year ago now—and she turned away before he could find out what she wanted. She was wearing a white dress and a white hat, and today she is wearing a tan dress and a straw hat. She has blond hair.

His hands are shaking. He steadies them against the *Missale Romanum* as he reads the gospel. "Thus far the word of the Lord," he says. She drove away in a little green Mustang, and he wonders what is troubling her. He will pray for her, and for Mandy and Rose. And Father Moriarty. And . . . and though he does not realize it, his mind drifts back to the mass and he is lost in it, and for a while at least he is delivered from the burden of being who he is.

†

Father Moriarty has soiled his sheets. He tried to hold it in, but Father LeBlanc had rushed out to say mass without coming to help him to the toilet, and now he's done it in his bed. Poor Father LeBlanc, he'll insist upon cleaning it up, getting fresh sheets, doing it all—he thinks—cheerfully. Poor bastard. And so are they all, poor bastards, poor banished children of Eve. Involuntarily Father Moriarty starts to pray, and his prayer drifts off into contemplation and he finds himself sitting at the foot of the cross, leaning his head against it, resting. It is all very peaceful. It is all as it should be. He lies there, stinking, in his own shit.

†

The bread has been consecrated and now the wine. Rose would like to lie next to him and fall asleep with her hand on his chest, right over his heart. Just that. Feel his heart beating in the dark.

†

Rose and Father LeBlanc are in the rectory kitchen. She has made toast for him and she has poured him coffee, and now, before she leaves for the day, she is making lunch for Father Moriarty. Tuna salad again. And another little can of Ensure in the fridge for his dinner.

"Why don't you sit down and have coffee with me?" Father LeBlanc says. He has never said this before.

Rose smiles at him, shaking her head no, and goes on preparing lunch.

Father LeBlanc finishes his toast and coffee and sits there looking at her. He is calm at last. Something happened during mass: a kind of peace descended on him, and in the interest of continued peace, he would like to resolve this matter with Rose. This miracle.

He is aware of the dangers of pride and presumption.

He is aware that God has selected her for his own good reasons.

He is aware that he has not been chosen.

"So, Rose," he says. She looks over at him. "So. It was a close call."

"Yes."

"We were overwrought, all of us."

"Yes."

"It was a close call for Mandy, though. Wasn't it."

"Yes."

"But not a miracle, I mean. She was never really dead or anything."

"No," she says.

"No," he says. "No way."

He gets up and puts his breakfast things in the dishwasher and turns to look at her. She does not look up.

"Take care," he says, and goes upstairs to check on Father Moriarty. But it was a miracle and they both know it. And he wants to get at it. He wants to get inside it. In Rose's heart. In her mind.

# FOUR

**THE DAYS ARE LONG AND OFTEN VERY HOT, BUT** at night there is always a cooling breeze off the ocean, which makes for perfect weather. It would seem that everyone is at peace in this small beach town. It's a funny little town, with a number of fishermen, some old Yankees who rent out cottages in the summer, a couple of schoolteachers, two nurses, Dr. Forbes, and a few kooks who just like to live here year-round. These are the natives, because you don't count people like the Carberrys or Sal or Nick Pappas—business owners—any more than you'd count the people who run the bank or the post office or the police department; they are natives, too, but they supply essential services and so they're different from real natives. And then there are the summer regulars who own beachfront homes and have kids, usually, and a nanny, and there's always a husband who comes up from Boston on the weekends. They certainly count. The summer regulars who rent the cottages that dot the narrow side streets from one end of the beach to the other—they count, too. People who stay at the motel right out of town don't count at all; they use the beach because the motel has bought beach privileges, but the guests come and go, and nobody ever gets to know them and nobody wants to. The real beach community is made up of the natives and the regulars who own or rent. Everybody knows everybody else, or at least they recognize one another and say hello, and everybody seems pretty peaceful. And why not? It's a peaceful place, the economy is good, and the weather is perfect. It is where Father LeBlanc has been sent into exile. For his own good.

†

Father Moriarty has been wondering how long it will take LeBlanc to get around to the so-called miracle. Less than a week, as it turns out.

"It was extraordinary," Father LeBlanc says. He is sitting beside Father Moriarty's bed, whispering, not looking at him. He tells how he tried to take Mandy's pulse and she had none; he is certain of that. "And Sal, the Clam Box guy, said she was dead, he's convinced, and Dr. Forbes, too . . ." But Father Moriarty interrupts and asks, "Was he sober? Forbes?" And Father LeBlanc continues, "He *was* sober, yes, and he pronounced her dead, officially. There is every evidence she was dead. I'm not exaggerating."

"And then all of a sudden she was alive?"

"Rose asked to be alone with her, with the body, and she sent us all out of the room, and the next thing we knew she was screaming 'No,' and she was crying, and later, when she opened the door, Mandy was alive. That's all."

"So what are you telling me? It's a miracle?"

Father LeBlanc says nothing; nor does he look up.

"Is that what you're saying?"

"I . . ." But he cannot say it.

"If it's a miracle, that's wonderful. That's fine for Rose. And for Mandy, I guess. But I wouldn't exactly put it in the parish bulletin yet, and I wouldn't bother passing on the news to His Holiness Paul the Sixth, gloriously reigning. Let it rest."

"I know. I know. It's just that I feel . . . involved somehow."

Father Moriarty closes his eyes. In LeBlanc's voice he hears something that sounds like spiritual greed. He thinks, and after a while he hears himself say, "If it really is a miracle, I don't see how it has anything to do with you."

Father LeBlanc is stung. "Maybe God is asking me for something."

"Maybe he's asking you to snap out of it. *That* would be a miracle."

There is a long silence in the room.

"What should I do?" Father LeBlanc asks.

"For Christ's sake, try thinking of someone besides yourself. Just for once."

Father LeBlanc flushes crimson. He says, "Thank you," and he leaves the room.

†

Father LeBlanc knows he should snap out of it, but still he wants to get inside this miracle, to know what Rose knows, to understand. This is why he stops in the kitchen each morning after mass. This is why he keeps trying to engage her in chat.

"Good coffee," he says. "Good toast, too."

Father LeBlanc never really noticed Rose before the miracle, but he has noticed her a lot since. He thinks of her each morning at mass. He prays for her during his thanksgiving after mass. And he watches her and tries to talk with her during his breakfast, which gets longer each morning. Before this Rose has always seemed the dutiful house-keeper, nice with Father Moriarty and thorough in her work around the place, but a stranger really. He looks at her: a small woman about his own age, dark hair, dark eyes, pleasant. A little overweight. Pretty, he supposes. He never thinks about women's looks; the promise of chastity leaves no room for window-shopping. He knows nothing about Rose. But he thinks about her constantly now that she has been chosen.

"Rose," he says. She looks up, expectant, but he has nothing to say. "How are you?"

"Fine."

"And Mandy? She's fine, too?"

"She's fine, too."

"Good, that's good," he says.

She pours him another cup of coffee.

"I know we agreed not to talk about it again, but—"

"I'll get you more half-and-half," she says.

"I have just a quick question, and I won't pry or anything, it's just that I need to know . . ."

"I'm fine," Rose says, "and Mandy's fine, too."

"But what *happened, Rose?"

Rose shakes her head. She will not talk about it.

"Just this one question. Just one word, yes or no. It was a miracle, wasn't it? Yes or no?"

The doorbell rings and Rose goes to answer it.

Father LeBlanc, defeated, puts his dishes in the washer. In a way, he expected something like this: the doorbell, the telephone, some kind of divine intervention that looks merely coincidental. Was it Freud who said there are no coincidences? It should have been Saint Paul; Paul always manages to put you in the wrong. Anyway, he *is* in the wrong. It was a miracle, period, and Rose has to live with it and he does not. Father LeBlanc goes up the stairs singing softly, "Summertime, and the . . . something . . . is easy."

†

"Is Father in? The young one?"

"Yes, but he doesn't see people before ten o'clock."

"But it's ten now."

It is that woman with the hat. She smiles as if something is funny, so Rose smiles back at her. "Come in," she says. She takes the woman's name—Annaka Malley—and seats her in the guest parlor while she goes back to the kitchen to get Father LeBlanc.

The woman looks familiar. At least her problem is familiar. Every summer they get somebody who looks like this one: rich and beautiful and spoiled. Even casually dressed, they seem ready for a party, and they're upset because their husband, who is in the city all week, has admitted he's got a girlfriend and wants out of the marriage. Or it's a man who has gotten himself into a summer affair, and now he wants to get out of it, and he figures the priest can help him. Rose doesn't know these things for a fact, but she watches television and she has eyes in her head and can see what they look like when they come knocking.

This one, she thinks, looks more like the girlfriend than the jilted wife.

Father LeBlanc is not in the kitchen and he's put his dishes in the washer, so he must have gone upstairs. He's probably in the toilet or brushing his teeth. Rose doesn't like the idea of knocking on his door right now, but what can she do? This is her job as housekeeper.

Maybe she's in luck and he's with Father Moriarty. She taps on Father Moriarty's door, which usually stands open during the day, and she puts her head inside.

"Oh, sorry."

His breviary is propped up in front of him on the tea rack and he is praying.

"I'm looking for the father," she says, apologizing.

"And what am I, chopped liver?"

"There's a lady to see him."

"Send her up to me. We'll give her a laugh."

Rose thinks for a second that this is a good idea. The woman might learn something about life from seeing the way Father Moriarty is dying. Rose gets one of those sudden surges of emotion she's been having lately, and tears come rushing to her eyes.

"Hey," he says. "I'm joking."

"I know that," she says crossly, "do you think I'm stupid?"

"I keep an open mind," he says.

Rose goes to Father LeBlanc's door and taps lightly on it. She taps once more, louder this time. She eases the door open a crack and sees he is at his prie-dieu. He is kneeling straight up, his hands folded, his head tipped back, his eyes wide open. "Excuse me," she says, but he does not turn to her. He does not hear anything, and as she stares at him she can tell he does not see anything either. He is not present at all. He is a saint.

She closes the door slowly, softly, and goes down the stairs.

In the guest parlor, she takes a deep breath and says to the woman, "Father is very busy just now. Do you suppose you could come back this afternoon?"

"I could wait."

"Well, the truth is, he's praying."

They exchange a guilty look, as if they have committed some violation of the priest's privacy.

"Oh, I'm sorry," the woman says, and Rose nods yes.

The woman leaves the rectory, embarrassed.

Rose aches for Father LeBlanc. And for Father Moriarty. And perhaps even for the woman.

✝

Monsignor Glynn is on one of his quick trips to see Father Moriarty, but he has decided to stay overnight and drive back to Boston in the morning. He has fed Father Moriarty his Ensure, and they have watched a rerun of *Barney Miller* together, and he sat by the bed until Father Moriarty fell asleep.

Now he is sitting in the guest room with Father LeBlanc. There is a bottle of bourbon on the desk and a saucer with a few melting ice cubes. They have been talking about Boston and about Vatican II and—dangerously—about the ordination of women. They don't agree on anything. They have been at it for nearly two hours and there is nothing left to say.

Father LeBlanc would like to tell Monsignor Glynn about the miracle, but instead he says, "Well, thanks for the drink."

"It's good for the soul, Paul."

They raise their glasses to each other, and Father LeBlanc pushes forward on his chair as if he is about to leave. He asks, "What do you think of Rose, Monsignor?"

"What do you mean?"

"I mean, how does she strike you?"

"Very nice woman. Tom thinks the world of her."

"Yes."

There is a long silence.

"Why?" Monsignor Glynn asks.

"She's just . . . there's something about her that . . ."

"Are you in love with her?"

Father LeBlanc sits back in his chair and blinks hard. "My God, you don't mess around, do you?"

"Didn't mean to startle you. It's just that she's young and you're young and you're both attractive and"—the monsignor wiggles his hands in the air like Dracula—"there's danger everywhere." He does an accent.

They laugh, and then they are silent for a moment.

"No, I'm not in love with her."

More silence.

"Have you ever been in love? With anybody?"

"No."

"It's not a crime, you know. It might even be a virtue."

"I've never let it happen. I've never let anyone inside."

"Ah, well."

"Have you? If I may ask? Since *you* ask."

"Yes, of course."

Father LeBlanc has nowhere to go with this, so he lifts his glass and discovers it is empty. Monsignor Glynn does not seem to notice.

"Three times. There was the high school girlfriend. There always is, and it's always real, or almost always. Then Tom, of course." Then he smiles to himself and says, "And this will kill you. The third one was the switchboard lady at the Kremlin. At the Kremlin! Three people is a lot."

"Tom? A man?"

"Tom Moriarty." He points upstairs. "That Tom."

Father LeBlanc goes red. He cannot imagine anyone in love with Father Moriarty.

Monsignor Glynn is amused. "You think men don't fall in love?"

"I know they fall in love. But in the priesthood, that's called sin. If I remember my canon law correctly."

"Oh, are you one of those simple souls who thinks that love necessarily leads to sex? There was no sex." Monsignor Glynn reflects for a moment. "There could have been sex—there *would* have been sex—with Maxine. The switchboard. But I saw where it was going, and I stopped it dead in its tracks."

"Maxine."

"I know. What a name. But a very good woman." He shakes his head.

Father LeBlanc again reaches for his empty glass, lifts it, then puts it back. Monsignor Glynn lights a cigarette. He smokes, and they are silent, thinking. In the distance they can hear the waves break softly on the beach. The tide is in. They are waiting for this to end.

"Are you okay?" Monsignor Glynn asks.

"I'm okay."

Father LeBlanc knows he should go, but he feels unable to. Everything seems suspended. Finally Monsignor Glynn stands up. "See you in a month," he says, "unless . . ." He means unless Father Moriarty dies before then. "Right?"

"Right."

"Okay, then."

"Okay."

"Oh, for God's sake, go to bed."

Father LeBlanc goes upstairs to his room and kneels by the window, trying to pray. He does not pray to be holy or even good. He prays without words: What do you want?

† 

Mandy is lying in bed listening to the harbor sounds and feeling good about herself. It's nice to be good. It's easy, too, at least after you've almost OD'd on coke and everybody is still more relieved than angry.

Her mother especially. Her mother is different this time, as if she's worried about something bigger than dying. It's too weird.

She can hear Sal downstairs in the Clam Box hollering at Luis, and she can smell the grease heating up for the fried clams and stuff, and it's sort of comforting to lie in bed while it all happens and you don't have to do nothing. Anything. There are shouts out in the harbor from the sailboat guys. The fishermen never holler. They don't have to holler because they know what they're doing, and besides they're making their living at this. They're not just having fun. She begins to hum a new Beatles song she heard last night at the Pit in Salisbury. It's real catchy. You're not supposed to be able to get into the Pit unless you're eighteen, but she can pass easily because she looks eighteen with her hair up, and anyhow she has a fake ID that says she's Jennifer Calamari, age nineteen, which she uses when she has to. But at the Pit, when they're really busy, they don't care much, and she shakes her ass a little bit and they smile and let her in. Last night she and Jake doubled with Cammie and Toom, and during one of the band's breaks, when they went out on the beach and stood around and stuff, she refused a toke, and they all laughed and teased her, but she didn't care. She folded her arms across her chest and began singing, "Hey, Jude, don't make it bad," and they all laughed like crazy and it was pretty funny. Afterward she felt good about it, and she still feels good about it now.

It isn't really addicting, despite what people say. Not marijuana and not coke either. You can have it like for recreation and then go off it and everything and then have like even more for recreation and still not be addicted. It's just one of those things old people tell you to scare you, to keep you from ever having a good time. That's all it is.

She feels very good. She feels sexy, in fact. She touches her breasts the way Jake likes to, but it's not the same when you do it yourself, so she stretches out full length, tightening all her muscles until they begin to hurt, and then she relaxes. She is Mandy Pandy, a good girl.

She thinks of calling Jake and telling him to come over. They could do it and then have breakfast—her mother always leaves coffee for her—and be out of here before Mama gets back from the priests'. Or she could call Cammie and they could talk about last night. Cammie and Toom haven't done it yet, or at least that's what Cammie says. She says she's saving herself for the boy she truly loves. Yeah, right. And who's that supposed to be when he's home, Mandy asked her once, and Cammie said she didn't know yet but she would when he came along. Meanwhile, Cammie said, I am quite content to remain a virgin. "I am quite content." That's exactly what she said. Cammie is nice though, anyhow. Maybe Cammie feels about being a virgin the same way she feels about refusing the toke. Maybe Cammie feels good about being good.

Mandy stretches once more and then lies with her hands folded behind her head. Life is unfathomable. "Unfathomable" is a new word she likes. Maybe she will do what her mother wants: finish high school, go to nursing school or maybe even college, *be* something. It's scary to think this way; what if she can't make it, what if she's not smart enough? She's never been that kind of a girl, reading books all the time and taking tests, and besides, she's got this great body. Right?

A gull shrieks outside her window as if it's agreeing with her. Unfathomable, she thinks. That seagull is unfathomable.

†

Father LeBlanc is making his thanksgiving after mass. Rose, he suddenly realizes, has loved her daughter back to life. That is the miracle.

†

Rose stands at the head of the stairs, not sure how to say it, not knowing how to begin.

"What?" It is Father Moriarty's voice.

She moves along the corridor and looks in at his door.

"What?" he says again. "What are you up to?"

"I wondered if you were sleeping or if maybe you wanted something."

"Come in," he says, and with a glance, he indicates the chair by the bed. "Come sit by me."

Rose enters the room and sits in the chair, leaning forward with one arm on the bed. Father Moriarty shifts around, or tries to, until his hand falls of its own weight and bumps against her arm. He puts his index finger on her wrist. They both smile. They remain that way for some time.

"Does it hurt?" Rose asks. "Are you in pain?"

He shakes his head no.

"No," she says.

She feels his finger on her wrist, and she thinks that, in a nice way, they are holding hands. She looks up at him and is surprised to see that his eyes are full of tears.

"What?" she says. "What is it?"

"I'm happy," he says. "Isn't that the damnedest thing?"

Her eyes too fill with tears.

"Now who's stupid?" she says.

She sits on the bed and bends over him until their foreheads touch, just for a moment.

She decides she will not tell him she is in love with Father LeBlanc.

†

Father LeBlanc is giving one of his dramatic homilies. He doesn't intend them to be dramatic; they just come out that way. He has been talking about Jesus raising Lazarus from the dead, and now he's winding up for the end.

"Lazarus is dead, four days dead and decaying in his tomb, and Jesus brings him back to life. Notice how the gospel of Saint John sets the scene. The mourners are gathered around the tomb. Mary and Martha are there, the two sisters of Lazarus who had sent for Jesus when their brother lay dying, but Jesus had not come to them. But now Jesus *is* here, too late, of course, because Lazarus is dead and buried. 'Roll back the stone,' Jesus says. They protest; Lazarus has been in the tomb for four days now; he is rotting, he stinks. Nonetheless they obey. They roll back the stone from the mouth of the tomb. And then, as they watch, wondering, Jesus raises his voice in a great cry: 'Lazarus, come forth,' he says, and—think of it, they're just like us, they cannot conceive of such a miracle— at Jesus' command the dead man comes out of the tomb, his hands and feet still wrapped in linen bands, his face wrapped in a cloth. Lazarus was dead and now he is alive. And Jesus says, simply, 'Loose him; let him go.'"

Father LeBlanc pauses.

"'How dearly he must have loved him,' the mourners said. Indeed Jesus loved Lazarus so much that he loved him back to life. He loves each of us in exactly the same way. He loves us back to life when we are dead."

There is silence in the church.

"On the last day we will be asked the only question that matters. Not were you good or bad. And certainly not were you successful, were you popular, were you rich. But this, only this: 'Whom have you loved back to life?'" He stops, a little dazed, because he has not intended to say this and in fact he is not sure what he has said. He repeats himself, slowly. "'Whom have you loved back to life when they were dead?'"

He doesn't know what to say next, and so he says nothing.

"In the name of the Father and of the Son and of the Holy Ghost, amen."

†

A week goes by. Nobody mentions his homily; everybody is embarrassed by it, he supposes. Certainly he is embarrassed by it. It was one of those things that seemed right at the time. His life, everything, is out of control, but for once it doesn't matter. He makes his meditation, he celebrates mass, he does the best he can. He is, in his way, happy.

†

The rectory parlor is gloomy despite the burnt-orange sofa and the tan-and-brown-striped chairs. In the late 1950s a modern-minded pastor furnished it from an office warehouse with teak and glass, and the decor has never been changed. It is a style Father Moriarty calls *la nouvelle Halloween,* but, appalled though he is by it, he has made no changes, aside from taking down the devotional artwork—a Sacred Heart and a Virgin Mary, sugary, both of them—and in their place hanging two soothing watercolors, an old barn in a field of mustard grass and a porch that looks onto a sunny view of the ocean. The rectory parlor is a strange place, when you think of it, he once said to Father LeBlanc: it's not meant to put you at ease; it's meant to take you completely out of your own world. Like purgatory. Or hell. Father LeBlanc thinks of this every time he has a visitor, and he thinks of it now. The visitor is that woman he's seen at mass.

He takes her in at a glance. She dresses simply, no jewelry, just a plain dress that cost plenty and a straw hat against the sun. She's very fair. She has short blond hair, thick, slightly waved, and she is very self-assured.

"I'm Father LeBlanc," he says. "The housekeeper tells me you stopped by a couple days ago."

"Yes," she says, and gives him a broad smile he does not return. It's a disarming smile, open and trusting, but he is on guard. She stops smiling. "Thank you for seeing me, Father."

"And you are?"

"Oh, I'm . . . my name is Annaka Malley."

He waits.

"I grew up in this parish. And I heard your sermon last week. The one on Lazarus?"

"Ah," he says. "And what can I do for you, Ms. Malley?"

Her tears start, he thinks, so he opens the drawer of the end table and takes out the box of tissues. He pushes it across the glass coffee table to her. She looks at it and looks at him and he sees he was mistaken. There are no tears.

"I thought the sermon was wonderful. I thought I'd tell you."

"Well, that's fine."

"Yes."

"And what is it you want to talk about?"

In fact there is nothing she wants to talk about. She has seen him saying mass and kneeling silently afterward, and he looked like a beautiful, tragic saint. But one Sunday as he finished mass and prepared to leave the altar, she saw him smile at the server, a new boy who had done everything wrong. She was surprised at the sudden animation of his face, the flash of white teeth, and she was astonished to find herself thinking, There is the man I could marry. Astonished most of all because he was a priest. And also because—since Devin—she was done with men. Furthermore, the idea was romantic and silly and she never thought that way. After that Sunday, however, she went to the rectory twice to talk to him. Once she met him on his way out of the house, and though he gave her that dazzling smile, he kept on going. And once she waited while the housekeeper went looking for him and came back to report that he was praying. She had felt like a criminal. But now she's back for a third time because she wants to talk to him. No, that's not true. She wants to be with him, to spend time with him, to get to know the smiling man inside the grim and saintly one, if only he'll come out. But it's clear he does not want to come out. And she is not supposed to be here, she understands, unless she has a problem.

"I guess I'm here on false pretenses. I don't have a problem. I just . . ."

He gives her a deliberate, patient look.

"Listening to your sermon on Lazarus, I thought . . . there's something in you that can help me understand."

"And that is?"

"Pardon?"

"That something in me that can help you understand? What is that?"

"Oh," and she blushes, "I didn't mean it to sound so awfully . . . intrusive. I didn't mean . . ."

He gives a hollow laugh. "And what is it you hope to understand?" He tries to stop himself, but it is too late. He is being overtly hostile, he is insulting, and he does not know why.

"I have a problem of faith," she says, lying. "I just wanted to talk with you. You—"

"What is it you want, Ms. Malley?"

She frowns and starts to speak and then stops. Her face, which has been open and trusting, suddenly closes against him.

"I want to leave," she says, standing up. "Thank you for your time."

He moves to get the front door for her, but she reaches it first and opens it herself.

"Thank you," she says again as she goes down the stairs.

He stands at the door watching her. He knows he has failed her. She came to him as a priest and he failed her. What the hell kind of priest is he? He wants to be a saint?

She gets in her car and drives away, fast.

†

Father LeBlanc is taking a new tack with Rose. He has realized suddenly that it isn't the miracle he has to understand; it's Rose herself.

He sees her every morning at mass and he sees her after mass while she makes breakfast for Father Moriarty and he sees her as much as he can on and off through the day. He has taken to walking her home after her morning's work because—as he explains, and it's partly true—he has a bone spur and can't run these days, and so he needs all the exercise he can get. Besides, he has errands at Carberry's.

Rose notices, however, that for once he's not wearing his priest's suit with the Roman collar; he's got on chinos and a yellow sport shirt and sneakers, which is how he dresses to work around the house. He never goes out like this. He looks very nice.

For a long time they walk in silence. The sun is hot but not too hot, and there is a light breeze.

"When you pray," he says finally, "how do you do it, exactly?"

Rose is embarrassed.

"I mean, are you conscious of praying?"

"I just say the Hail Mary, usually."

"Ah."

"And sometimes I try to say the rosary, but to tell the truth, my mind wanders and I start worrying about Mandy or selfish things, like money or getting the car fixed, or I think of the soap operas. *The Young and the Restless.* I watch it whenever I can."

"Yes."

"I don't pray very much."

"Hmm."

"I'm not a very good person. I'm a sinner."

"We're all sinners," he says. "Not all of us have miracles."

They walk in silence again.

They pass one of the tide pools, a patch of black water thick with lily pads. There is a sweetish smell in the air. They stop to look at the pool, and after a while Rose picks up a small stone and lobs it into the water. It makes a loud plop, and at once any number of frogs, invisible until now, jump from the bank with that indignant croaking sound they make. Father LeBlanc laughs. He is a city boy and is still surprised by things like this.

"There's a lily," he says, pointing. "Look."

"There's lots of them," she says. "They smell like gardenias, almost."

Father LeBlanc takes off his sneakers and his socks, rolls his chinos up to his knees, and wades out into the water. It is mushy on the bottom and his feet sink into the ooze. He hates the feel of it, but he moves steadily toward the nearest lily. His pants are getting wet. He reaches out and grabs the lily just beneath the blossom and pulls it toward him. He lifts it from the water, but the stem doesn't break off; it seems to go on forever, a long green cord attached to the center of the earth.

"Look at this," he says. "Look at this thing!"

"That's how they are," she says, laughing at him.

He twists the stem free and wades back to the shore, the lily raised high in his hand. He climbs the bank and presents her with the flower. He makes a little bow.

"*Gracias, señor,*" she says, bending her knee in a mock curtsy.

They laugh, and then they are both embarrassed, so he busies himself rolling down his wet pant cuffs, shuffling into his socks and sneakers. She twirls the flower between her fingers.

"What a mess," he says. "I'm soaking wet."

She watches him stoop to tie his laces, the curve of his back, his hairy arms, those thick legs. He is a handsome man and he is very sexy. She turns away and says, "It's going to be a scorcher today."

"But it's nice now," he says.

"Yes," she says, "this is very nice."

On the way home he sings "Red Roses for a Blue Lady," a ridiculous song he hasn't even thought of since high school.

†

She has made the bed and dust-mopped the whole apartment, and now, as Rose comes through the door, Mandy is sponging down the kitchen counter.

Rose smiles and gives her a little kiss. "My good girl," she says. "My Mandy Pandy."

"How's that," Mandy says, pointing to the counter, "and look at this," as she leads her mother into the living room and then the bedroom. "Dust-mopped, the bed made, what do you think?"

"I think you're a wonderful girl."

"Right."

"I think you can do anything you put your mind to. Finish high school, go to nursing school, even college, whatever you want."

"Oh, Ma."

"All you have to do is buckle down, excetera. *Et*cetera."

"Don't start, Ma, please."

"I'm not starting. I'm just saying."

"See, that's why I hate to do anything around this place. I do one little thing and then you start in on me. It's high school and then it's college or a nursing degree. It's always something more. Jeez."

"I only want you to be happy."

"Then leave me alone, why don't you!"

"Mandy, come on."

"I'm going out. I'm gonna hang out with Cammie."

"But not with Jake, Mandy. Not him, please."

"I don't see Jake anymore, I told you that. I see Cammie. My God, I've gotta have *some* friends. I'm not an old maid yet, like some people."

"Have a good time, sweetie. Do you need some money? Here, take a couple dollars."

"Whatever," Mandy says, and takes the money and goes out.

Rose moves slowly to the window and sits down. She's a hypocrite, pretending to the father that she says the rosary and at the same time wishing she could put her hand on his chest and his shoulders and all over him. His ass. She shakes her head to stop thinking like this. It is Mandy she should be thinking about.

†

Annaka Malley has been attending daily mass off and on for the past two weeks, and she is finally getting used to the church again. It is homely, welcoming, a wood-frame building with a vaulted ceiling where all the rafters are exposed. Everything is painted a cream color, and even the stations of the cross are cream colored. There is no brightness anywhere, except from the windows, which are not really glass but some kind of heavy plastic tinted a dull red and blue and yellow, the kind of stuff you see as booth dividers in bars and restaurants all along the coast.

This is the church she attended every Sunday as a girl, back when she was Anna Kathryn Malley, dressed in her best clothes and sitting between her mother and father, wondering if everyone knows about them. She is pretty and popular and always in a good mood, but there is a part of her—her secret life—that nobody knows. She never invites anybody to her house, and when she goes to the movies or down to Salisbury, she always meets her friends at the bus stop or at their houses or anywhere but at home. It is because of her mother and father. Ever since she can remember, they have quarreled—their voices low, terrible—and sometimes they have gone for days without speaking; but one night something happened and since then they have not spoken to each other at all. She has no idea what was said, but whatever it was, it was unforgivable. They speak through Anna Kathryn now—"Tell your father his dinner is ready" and "Tell your mother I've eaten my dinner"—and there is nothing she can do about it. She has asked her mother, "Please, why won't you talk to him," but her mother squinted hard at her and said, "So? You're taking his side?" And when she asked her father, he looked away and said, "It's none of your business." At school she is alive, but at home there is no space for living. She has made a firm resolution: when she grows up and gets out of this place, she will never marry.

Once, working in the garden with her father, she pulled up some weeds with purple flowers and said, "Look how pretty," and he said, "Here, make a bouquet and take them in to your mother." She was excited, hopeful for a moment, and she ran to the house with the bouquet. She found her mother sitting in the darkened bedroom. "These are for you," she said, "Daddy said to give them to you." Her mother turned and looked at her as if she were a stranger. "What are they?" she asked. Then she caught her breath and pushed the flowers away. "They're purple," she said, "they're death flowers. Get them out of this house." And she screamed, "Get out! Get out!" Anna Kathryn went to the cellar then and crouched down next to the water heater. She tried to cry but found she couldn't, and so she sang, quietly, all the songs she learned at school. An hour passed, and when she went out to her father, he already knew. Before she could tell him anything, he looked away and laughed, a short sour laugh.

It has been this way for seven years, the silence at meals, the heavy, unbreakable silence that clings to the curtains and the wallpaper and the carpets. She cannot breathe in this house. She goes to movies with her friends, she goes to dances and she acts in the school plays, and at these times she is smart and funny and she flirts with everybody. They're always glad to see Anna Kathryn. But at home she is silent and frightened, and she aches.

This is what she remembers of Sunday mass, this living death. She sees this death in Father LeBlanc. She should flee from him, she knows. But there's also something alive and wonderful inside him, and she is drawn to that, drawn irresistibly, despite herself.

She kneels in church, Our Lady of Victories, and she follows the mass and decides yet again that today she will speak to him, this Father LeBlanc. She does not want to, but she feels she must.

But once again she loses her nerve.

†

Mandy opens the heavy glass door of the Clam Box and gets hit with the late morning smells of the place: hot grease, clams, fish chowder, corn on the cob; it's all mixed in together. Luis is pitching clamshells into a metal trash can. Sal is dragging a twenty-gallon vat of something out of the pantry and then humping it across the cement floor. What a shit house.

Mandy stands inside the door and looks around. Sure enough, Jake is in his corner.

"Hey," she says.

Jake says nothing, but Sal finishes with his vat and greets her from behind the counter. "Hey," he says, laughing, "how's the dead girl!"

She makes a face at him and slips into the chair across from Jake. "Christ," she says, "I can see I'm gonna be real popular around here once I'm dead."

"Hey," Jake says.

"So what are you on?"

"Just grass," he says. He stares at her as if he means to say something, but she can see he's forgotten already.

"What, for Chrissake?"

"Have you tried for the car?"

"Are you kidding? After the accident, you think she's gonna give me the car?"

"You could ask her."

"Yeah, right."

"You could do it for me."

He gives her that crooked grin she can never resist. She puts her hand on his arm, and with the other hand she reaches under the table and touches his crotch. They are in love.

†

Annaka Malley likes the privacy of daily mass. She is one of seven or eight parishioners, all of them apparently strangers to one another and happy to remain so. That suits her fine.

Today she waits until mass is done and everyone leaves the church, which they do very quickly, and then she goes down the aisle, genuflects before the altar, and approaches the sacristy door. She has never been in the sacristy and doesn't know what to expect. The door is open and she looks in. A green linoleum floor, a kitchen sink with a cabinet above it, a row of closets—for vestments, she supposes—and over in the corner a kneeler and a chair and, incongruously, a gallon jug of white wine.

Father LeBlanc is standing at a table, putting his mass vestments on a heavy wooden hanger. She knocks on the door frame to catch his attention, but he seems lost in thought and does not look up. She clears her throat. She knocks again. As she is about to turn away, Father LeBlanc notices her and smiles warmly. She did not expect that smile.

"Come in, come in," he says, and he hangs the vestments in the long closet by the vesting table. He is wearing only a T-shirt and black pants, and to her he looks half-undressed, but he doesn't seem to notice. He takes his cassock from the same closet and climbs into it. "How are you? I'm glad you've come back."

She is flustered, but this time she is prepared.

104

"I have to apologize for the other day," she says. "I shouldn't have walked out like that. It was very rude."

"No problem," he says. "I'm the one who should apologize. I was distracted, I think. I must have been distracted."

She laughs softly for no reason.

"No, I wasn't distracted. The truth is, I was terrified because I have problems of faith, too, and I don't know how to talk about them. I've never talked about them." He stops, then he goes on. "I pray for faith. And sometimes, when that seems too much to ask, I just pray for hope."

She was prepared, but not for this. What can she say?

"I'm sorry," he says. "I shouldn't intrude my . . ."

"No, no," she says. "Yes."

He gives a little laugh, and she laughs too.

"Can I come and talk to you? Today?"

"I've got the prison today. Tomorrow?"

"Tomorrow."

"Tomorrow morning at ten?"

"Tomorrow morning at ten."

She smiles and he smiles and, uncertain how to end this, she shakes his hand. She leaves the sacristy and walks out past the altar and down the front aisle of the church. She goes to her car. She is happy. She is elated. Tomorrow she will tell him everything. She will pour out her soul to him. They'll be friends. He will love her.

She stops herself. That's just sentimentality.

What will happen is this: she won't pretend she has a problem of faith, she will simply tell him about her life—the men, the failures—and perhaps he will help her to see it differently. Maybe even to do something about it. But that's all.

It is important to stick to facts.

†

Father Moriarty is feeling very peppy these days, he says, and Mrs. Schwartz says she's glad to hear it. She asks him what "peppy" can possibly mean for someone like him, and he thinks about it while she changes the sheets, rolling him from one side of the bed to the other and then back again. Propped up between his new sheets, he says, "I guess it means that if I could, I'd take a long drive up the coast to Maine and I'd park on a cliff and watch the ocean. Then I'd buy a hot dog with French's yellow mustard, the really cheap kind, and a big root beer, and then I'd drive home."

"Well," she says, "if you're that peppy, you ought to take advantage of it. I could drive you up the coast, or that other priest could, or Rose."

He ponders this. Mrs. Schwartz has always been as distant as one person can possibly be from another whom she washes and tosses around in bed and generally treats like a misbehaving child. He thought it was because he is a priest, and she is a Jew and uncomfortable around priests, but maybe he's had it all wrong. Maybe she didn't much like him and now she does. Or maybe a fit of charity has attacked her and he should encourage it. Or, who knows, maybe it's one of the little surprises that make up his days, a little love note from God, if there is a God.

"Well," Mrs. Schwartz says, "what do you say? If you think you're up to it, I'd be glad to give you a hand. I'm sure Dr. Forbes will say okay."

"But I'm mostly dead."

"Mostly but not completely."

"I'll think about it."

"Just say the word," she says. And she adds, as if she is the first person to have the thought, "We mustn't let fear get in the way."

†

They're in the kitchen after mass. Father LeBlanc is eating his breakfast and Rose is messing around the kitchen, bursting to talk, he can tell.

"Well, what?" he asks.

"I'm feeling so good," Rose says. "Mandy is doing great, no drugs, no drinking, and she's not seeing that Jake. She's even helping around the house. I feel good."

"Did you have a firm talk with her, or what?"

"No! No, that's the thing. For once I didn't nag at her, I was so relieved to have her back, and I guess that was the right thing to do."

"Well, that's good."

She touches his hand. "I'm so happy," she says. "Thank you."

Father LeBlanc is on his guard today. He went too far yesterday when he walked Rose home—that business with the water lily. He was trying to draw her out, to get a glimpse into her interior life at the place where her prayer begins, but he must have lost his direction, and instead of drawing her out, he was . . . seducing is much too strong a word . . . but he was playing up to her, personally, almost sexually. The lily. That was going too far. Looking back, he can see that it just happened, it was a spontaneous thing he might have done anytime in his life, to shuck off the old sneaks and jump into the pond. But with a girl, a woman, it's different, especially when you pick a flower and present it to her with that stupid bow. He blushes, remembering it. He's got to be more careful. Rose sees him blush and pulls her hand away.

"That woman is at mass every day, I notice," Rose says. "The one who came here to see you three days ago, four, whatever it was. In the hat."

"Yes."

"She's a beautiful woman." Rose pauses and then goes on, quickly. "Always so beautifully dressed. She's from here, you know. From this parish, even though she doesn't look it. More coffee? No? Her father died right before you came here. You didn't know him. Michael Malley."

Father LeBlanc nods. He is thinking of Rose and that miracle.

"Suicide." She draws her finger across her throat. "He hung himself."

"Oh." He has heard about this. There was some flap about whether to bury him in consecrated ground, but Father Moriarty had insisted on doing it.

"He lost his wife, and a month later he killed himself. It's kind of a love story." She looks up at him, but he does not respond— maybe he doesn't like this kind of talk—so she changes the subject. "Father Moriarty is feeling very peppy these days, he says. He says that Mrs. Schwartz offered to take him for a drive up the Maine coast and get him a hot dog. Can you believe he wants a hot dog?"

"I don't think he wants a hot dog."

"That's what she said, Mrs. Schwartz, a hot dog. He's not well enough to get in a car and drive, if you ask me. He doesn't eat anything, hardly; it's only the Ensure that keeps him alive. How could he get in a car? When you help him with the toilet, it takes so much out of him that he falls asleep right afterward. How is a man like that supposed to drive to Maine? I don't understand this Mrs. Schwartz."

"She's a nurse. I suppose she knows what she's doing."

"Nurse's aide."

He is not listening. He drinks his coffee, folds his hands, and looks beyond her into space. "When you pray, Rose, at mass, do you follow the words in the missal, or do you just think, or do you let your mind go sort of blank?"

"I just try to pay attention."

"And how do you *feel*? I don't mean feeling good or bad. What I mean is: are you aware of something happening inside you?"

She looks at him as if she has no idea what he is talking about. "To your soul?"

"I think you've got the wrong idea about me, Father. I go to mass because I promised the Virgin I would go every day if Mandy didn't die. And she didn't die. So I go."

He nods. "Yes," he says.

There is a long silence and then Rose asks, casually, "Are you walking into town today, Father?"

"I'm not sure," he says. "It depends on how long I'm at the prison."

But he does walk her into town and they do not stop at the lily pond and he does not offer her a flower. They are priest and house-keeper once again, except that they walk together intimately, like old friends. And Rose feels good enough to dance.

†

Father Moriarty has been meditating on fear. Sometimes grace comes in just this way: Mrs. Schwartz suddenly says, "We mustn't let fear get in the way," and immediately you know this is a message sent directly to you, as clear and pointed as anything Saul ever got from the Witch of Endor. And perhaps more troublesome. Fear has been his whole life, really. The smart talk, the so-called honesty, even the brave front he puts on this final, fatal disease—"amyotrophic lateral sclerosis, mine, not Lou Gehrig's"—is a way of dealing with fear. What kind of person would he have been if he'd dropped these layers of self-protection and let himself be exposed for the poor fool he is? Frightened and finite and, like any of us, breakable in twenty seconds? Would he have been a priest at all? Would he be saying things like "Thank God, if there is a God"? He pauses. Is he being too hard on himself? No, this is truth. It comes from Mrs. Muriel Schwartz, home-help indeed.

†

Annaka Malley arrives the next day at ten, promptly, for her talk with Father LeBlanc. She looks around the little parlor while she waits for him to appear, and she is surprised to see that it's more like a dentist's office than a priest's. At least there are no old magazines stacked on the end tables. Just a box of tissues and, surprisingly, an ashtray. The tissues were in the drawer last time; now they're on top of the table, within easy reach. Does this mean something?

She looks up as the door opens and Father LeBlanc comes in. She stands and they shake hands.

"It's good to see you," he says, but his face looks grim and determined.

"Well, thank you for making time for me."

"Not at all. Not at all."

She has been looking forward to this, but now she is confused. He was so warm and friendly when they talked in the sacristy, but here in his own parlor he is cold and distant. They are silent for a moment, and then both talk at the same time.

"Do you want to just tell me—?"

"Can I just tell you—?"

"You first," he says.

"All right. Okay. I mentioned that I have a problem of faith, but that's not strictly true, I'm afraid. The problem is more, well, personal."

"Yes."

"Yes." She's going to forge ahead. "It's just that I've seen a shrink, a psychiatrist about this . . . two, in fact, at different times, of course . . . so I know . . . well, knowledge has never changed anything, has it . . . The fact is that I can't keep a relationship. I get involved, and as soon as I get involved, I get afraid and I pull away. I've lived with three different men in the last ten years, and every time we get to the marriage question, I pull away. I know why, but I'm not able to do anything about it."

"Yes," he says, and waits. "That *is* something you'd want to talk to a psychiatrist about, isn't it." He speaks in his priest voice, precise, distancing. "It's disturbing, to be sure, but it's not a problem of faith."

"Not faith in God, no. But it makes marriage impossible. And it doesn't do much for your sense of self."

"Self," he says. "Again a problem that's more appropriate for a psychiatrist than a priest."

She looks at him. He's all priest, that's for sure. That other man—the one with the smile, the human one—where did he go? Meanwhile, this one continues.

"Faith is a kind of desperate hold on things. It means a life apart. It means a life of loneliness." He talks more slowly, more quietly.

"It can demand of us the dark night of the senses—of the intellect—where faith is reduced to hope and you don't know who you are or where you are."

It sounds to her like marriage.

"You might ask if God actually wants that for anyone, and I have to believe it's so. Not just saints and mystics, but even people who simply aspire to sanctity. To goodness, I mean."

There is a knock at the door, and Rose asks if they would like coffee? Or tea? Or anything at all? Annaka Malley says no and Father LeBlanc says no and Rose goes away.

"It sounds inhuman," Annaka says. "Faith."

He goes on, but she stops listening. She hears only occasional words: desperate . . . contradiction . . . loneliness . . . cold . . . and she thinks, Who can bear any of this? His voice drifts. She feels he is talking from a great distance and the words are not really spoken but transmitted somehow, like a bad phone connection. He pauses, and she remembers he is talking about faith.

Faith in God, as he tells it, is worse than home life with the Malleys. It's only his smile that makes him seem human.

She waits for the smile, but it does not come. It's all too much, and so she stands and says, "Thank you, Father," and before he even has time to feel foolish, she is gone.

† 

Father LeBlanc feels raw, stripped of everything, even his flesh. He wants God to love him, he wants only to be a saint. He kneels down beside his bed and covers his face in shame. Black butterflies beat around his head.

†

Father Moriarty is on his way to Pinnacle Rock at the end of Rosary Lane. He is twenty-seven, a seminarian, and it is night. He is supposed to be in his cubicle getting ready for bed, but suddenly he couldn't stand the closeness of all those other seminarians, the certainty and the quiet and the hothouse spirituality, so he put his cassock on over his pajamas and walked out of the dormitory into the dark.

It is cool outside, there is only a sliver of moon, and he walks rapidly across the grass till he reaches the lane. It is called Rosary Lane because every morning at eleven they have a study break when all the seminarians, in bands of three, say the rosary as they walk from the main building to Pinnacle Rock at the end of the lane and then back again. The walk is just long enough to say a good devotional rosary, unless you get some idiot in your band who insists on speeding up and getting everybody out of sync. This is the first time Father Moriarty—but he is only Tom Moriarty now, a seminarian—has walked this path alone.

He stands on Pinnacle Rock and looks out over the valley. There are night sounds of birds and small animals, there is the sharp smell of pine in the air, and in the dark he can see the shifting shapes of trees and bushes far below him. It is cold. He has come out here to think, to face some hard truths, and the truth he has chosen to face is that soon he will have nothing except God, because love is incomprehensible and nothing matters except the love of God. Friends, yes, Ed Glynn, certainly, but God only.

Below him in the valley, the night sounds grow louder, small scurrying animals, wee timorous beasties.

He will be ordained to the priesthood in less than a month, and then his life will be—for all personal purposes—over.

He looks down into the night valley and thinks, Do I really believe in God? At once all his defenses rush in, conscience gets in his way, and he finds himself praying blindly, but still he forces himself to think, What if there is no God? What if he is just the shadow of my fear of being alone?

He turns back to the seminary and his known and quiet cubicle, and he absolutely refuses to wonder, Have I faced it?

Years later, however, he will wonder.

†

When Rose gets home she finds that Mandy has cleaned the apartment and set the table for lunch. She has even put paper napkins beside their plates. "You relax," she tells her mother, "and I'll go downstairs and get the clam rolls." She returns five minutes later with a white sack, clam rolls and tartar sauce and a half-pint of Sal's super potato salad.

"Nice," Rose says, and they look out over the harbor and eat their lunch in silence. Rose has nothing to say—she is tired and happy—and Mandy is waiting until the time is right.

Finally they finish their lunch.

"Don't you get tired walking to work every day?" Mandy asks. "You walk all that way and then you clean their house and then you have to walk all the way back."

"It's good exercise."

"But then you have to work for Sal from six to eleven."

"Five to eleven, but not every day."

"See what I mean? And you could save yourself, you know?"

"By driving, you mean."

"Well, yeah."

"If I get the car out of the shop, you mean. Right?"

"Well, it's not that big of a deal! I mean, how much could it cost to have it fixed? I've got to learn to drive anyhow. I've got to take driver's ed this year at school, and if you got the car out, I could practice. I could even drive you to work and pick you up."

"Without a license."

"Well, that would be after I learned. I could shop for you. I could do errands. I could drive myself to school so I wouldn't have to hang around waiting for that bus. It would be safer too."

"I don't think so, Mandy. I think we'd better wait on the car."

"Suit yourself," Mandy says, and begins to clear the table. When she is almost done, she says, "I can always get a ride to school with Jake. On his motorcycle." Rose does not respond. "But it doesn't matter," Mandy says, "just so long as you're happy. See ya!"

She has somehow made this sound like a threat, but before Rose can think of anything to say, Mandy is out the door and gone.

†

Annaka Malley parks her car but doesn't get out. Once again, despite her resolutions, she has gone to see Father LeBlanc after mass, and once again she has made an appointment to talk with him privately. For some reason—and it is not just his looks—she can't help herself.

She is wearing a yellow linen dress, loose-fitting, and she knows she looks good in it. She is wearing tan sandals, a tan straw hat. She is not dressing for him, she is sure of that. Not that he would notice anyhow.

It's after ten and she is going to be late, but she cannot bring herself to get out of the car and go into the rectory. It is too depressing. *He* is too depressing. She looks over at the rectory just as the door opens and Father LeBlanc looks out. He has on that grim face. She waves at him and he waves back, puzzled as she starts the car and turns slowly toward home. She drives. And then, without actually deciding to, she pulls onto the freeway and continues on toward Boston.

This is it. She has made up her mind. She will never see Father LeBlanc—or his depressing God—again. Not in this life.

†

In her dream Rose opens the door to Father LeBlanc's room and slips inside. She does not close the door—which she knows is dumb, she knows it is fatal—and she does not wait for her eyes to adjust to the dark. Swiftly she moves across the room, blind but surefooted, and stands at the door to his bathroom. She can hear the shower running and she thinks she can hear him singing. She eases the bathroom door open a crack. At once the bedroom is flooded with light. She is exposed here, visible from the corridor and visible from the bathroom as well, but still she does not move. She is determined to see him and to hold him. Father LeBlanc gets out of the shower and begins to dry himself off. He has a mat of black hair on his chest, and he is hairy below as well; his arm muscles swell and jump beneath the skin as he dries his chest and then his legs and then his private parts. She looks at him. She wants to take him in her hands, to touch him all over, she wants to taste the salt in the hair on his chest. She is wearing only her nightgown, but when she looks down, she discovers the nightgown lies at her feet and she is naked. She takes a step toward him and he looks up. He smiles at her. There is a sound behind her and she turns to see Father LeBlanc, but now he is wearing his black gown and his clerical collar, and he is frowning. He is very sad. "No," he says, and he is shaking his head. "Such an easy, stupid sin," he says. She picks up the nightgown at her feet and covers her breasts with it. She does not know what to do. This is a dream, she realizes, and it is not for her to decide what happens next. At once he is beside her, naked again, and he pulls her close and whispers in her ear. "Rose," he says, "Rose," and they sink to the floor and begin to make love.

She wakes.

She has had a terrible dream—she can't remember what—and her head aches and all her joints are stiff. She feels rotten. She says a Hail Mary and then she drags herself out of bed and goes off to take a shower. Another day.

†

Father LeBlanc is accompanying Rose to Don's Auto Body, which is located in the pine woods out behind Carberry's. Don has been looking at the car for a couple months now, and sometimes he has fiddled with it, but mostly he has ignored it. It's just part of the junk that covers the acre lot where he lives and works and drinks his beer. Rose called him earlier this week and told him that she needs the car for a trip to Maine, so he got serious and sent for parts and now it's ready. Father LeBlanc's notion is that Don won't try to overcharge her if she's got a man with her.

They're walking slowly today because it's hot. They haven't much to say, it's just a companionable walk, side by side, their shoulders bumping now and then, or their arms, and they are very happy. When they get to the lily pond, Father LeBlanc stoops and picks up a flat stone and scales it across the water. At once the crickets begin to shrill their warnings, the frogs plop heavily into the water, the cicadas whir. Father LeBlanc smiles and looks over the dark water, satisfied, as if he has accomplished something.

"Thanks, Mrs. Calabash, wherevah you are!"

"Who's that one?" Rose asks.

"Jimmy Durante," Father LeBlanc says, but before he can explain, a motorcycle begins its approach, grinding loudly even at a distance, and they watch as it gets closer, picking up speed, shifting into high gear, and then in less than a second it speeds past. Jake is driving the motorcycle and Mandy clings to him from behind. She waves at them and laughs, a mocking laugh.

Rose and Father LeBlanc continue on to Don's Auto Repair. They pick up the car and Don gives her a special price, he says. "Our reward is in heaven, right, Father?" And he winks at Rose.

That afternoon as Rose goes down to work in the Clam Box, she meets Mandy on the stairs. Mandy is flushed, tanned, and she says in that way of hers, "Saw you with your boyfriend." She laughs thinly, but her laugh seems to go on for a long time.

†

Father Moriarty is going for a ride. Rose has volunteered to drive him to Maine and buy him that hot dog and he has said yes, let's do it.

Father LeBlanc carries him down the stairs and props him up in the front seat with pillows and a blanket. He pulls the seat belt out as far as it will go and tightens it carefully across Father Moriarty's chest and waist and the mountain of padding that's holding him together. He tucks the old priest's thumbs under the seat belt to keep his hands from falling.

"What do you think?" he asks Father Moriarty. "Do you think you'll be all right?"

"We mustn't let fear get in the way," Father Moriarty says.

"Thus spake Muriel Schwartz."

"I wouldn't mind going along, you know. Then I wouldn't have to worry about you two."

"You'll worry until a week after you're in the grave, Paul. It's your nature. Rejoice in it."

Rose stands beside the car, quiet and a little desperate.

"But is this prudent?" Father LeBlanc asks.

"Prudence is the ugly stepsister of incapacity," Father Moriarty says. "That's a quote. From somebody. Now I'm all out of one-liners, so let's go."

They set off up the coast in silence, Rose concentrating on the highway and Father Moriarty gazing out over the water. It is a perfect day for a ride. The sun is high, there is a light breeze, the water is deep green. They don't talk, though now and then Father Moriarty says things to himself that seem to be from the Scriptures or something. "Death by water," he says, and a long time later, "By the rivers of Babylon, there we sat down and wept when we remembered Zion." And then, peppy, "How ya doing, Rose?" In a short while they reach Portsmouth and he says, "I'm beginning to fade a little, Rosie. I wonder if we should get that hot dog pretty soon. Sometime, say, before I drop dead."

She gets him the hot dog, with French's yellow mustard, and a large root beer. They drive to a headland and park the car looking out over the water.

"It's every color," he says, his eyes closed. "What a sight."

"It's green," she says.

He does not touch the hot dog.

They turn back and reach home in less than an hour. Rose is wondering why they have done this. Why this preposterous trip, the exhaustion, the disturbing silence? As they turn up Church Lane, Father Moriarty says to her, in a voice thinned by fatigue, "You're a good woman, Rose. You know that."

She reaches over and touches his hand.

Father LeBlanc is waiting out front.

"Thank heavens," he says, and wonders why the two of them look so different, as if—he thinks jealously—as if they have seen God.

†

Father LeBlanc is meditating before mass. He kneels at his prie-dieu, his face in his hands, trying to fix his vision on the crucified Christ. Storm clouds are gathering in the gray sky, and there is the clank of armor as the soldiers throw dice to see who will get his seamless robe. No one is weeping. The women stand, silent, awful, waiting for it to be over. The men have slunk away, as men always do. And he is kneeling there, his hands over his face, trying to see into the crucified Christ. He only wants what God wants for him.

He keeps his eye on Christ, but he thinks of that morning—it seems ages ago—when he made the offer: Whatever you want, I'll give it. Anything. And he knows, as he knew then, that a bargain has been struck. Not sanctity, not happiness, but God's implacable will. Then the miracle happened, and since then his life has been chaos. Rose. And Annaka Malley. And Rose. He is bothered by Annaka Malley—he failed her and she seems to have dropped out of his life—but he is obsessed by Rose.

†

"Well, I'm going with him and too bad about you!" Mandy slams the door and dashes down the stairs to the parking lot where Jake is waiting for her.

Rose follows her to the head of the stairs. She watches while Mandy gets on the motorcycle, hoping she'll turn around and wave good-bye, but she just tosses back her hair and they speed away. "Mandy," Rose says, almost to herself, and then she goes inside and slams the door behind her. What can you do with that girl? She is hopeless.

Mandy presses her body hard against Jake's as they tear along the winding ocean road. There is fog tonight, no moon, and the road and the sky seem all one. Living like this is great: the wind from the ocean, a kind of moisture in the air that's wet and sexy, and this powerful thing roaring between your legs. You're with someone you love, you're picking up speed, you're getting away, getting the hell out of here, for good. This is the life.

They round a hairpin turn, leaning to the left, leaning and leaning until it seems they're bound to wipe out, and then they snap upright again, and the pressure sends them bouncing high on the seat, and Mandy laughs with pleasure, with exultation.

She loosens her hold on Jake just as they go into another turn, too sharp, and the cycle skids wildly with a screeching sound and the smell of burning. What a rush! What a thrill! And then suddenly the cycle tumbles over and over, and Mandy rises in the air, in slow motion, her brown hair blowing up and away from her head as she spins once in a giddy somersault and lands softly in the sand by the side of the road. Her head hits first, the back of her head, and she makes a grunting sound, surprised, as the rest of her body slumps to the sand and bounces once, and again, her neck snapping with a dull sound, and then she rolls over and lies very quiet.

# FIVE

THERE IS QUIET EVERYWHERE. WAVES SLIDE UP THE
beach silently and trickle back. Frogs and crickets and the small night
animals make no sound. In the distance an owl hoots once, softly,
then silence hangs heavy as the fog. For a long moment the smell
of gasoline taints the air, and then a breeze rises, and the sharp smell
of seaweed follows, and the smell of honeysuckle. No one passes
along the beach road where Mandy is lying dead, her eyes open,
and where Jake lies, hoping none of this has happened. After a while
the breeze becomes a soft wind and sweeps away the fog, reveal-
ing a hard gray sky and a white moon. Jake watches as a dark cloud
approaches the moon, drifts in front of it, passes on. He feels nothing, not in his arms or legs, and he cannot move, and he cannot
call for help. He does not want to think about Mandy.

Out on the highway a car goes by, and then another. A long
time passes and finally a pickup truck slows down at the sight of the
overturned motorcycle, and then it speeds up and disappears from
sight. But apparently the driver notifies the police, because a few
minutes later they appear. The two policemen establish at once that
Mandy is dead—a broken neck and God knows what else, the young
one says—and that Jake is in some kind of shock. They know him
from the Vets Hospital.

"Hey, Jake," the older one says. "Are you alive, shithead?"

And the other says, "Can you move? Can you stand up?"

Jake grunts and tries to speak.

"What?"

Jake says something about speaking.

"Didn't anybody ever teach you to enunciate. E-nun-ci-ate!" The older cop has no patience.

"I think I'm paralyzed. I can't even speak."

"Yeah, well, you solved that problem, at least. You're coming in nice and clear. Can you move your foot?" The cop gives Jake's foot a little nudge with his boot.

"Hey!" Jake says, and shifts his leg.

"How's your neck?" They test it. "Your arms? Shoulders?" They decide he's just too scared to move, so the older one says, "Try to stand up. Here, we'll help you."

They slip their arms under him and slowly lift him to a sitting position.

"How are you so far?"

"Mandy?" Jake asks. "Is she okay?"

They don't answer.

"Is she gonna be okay?"

"We called the ambulance. They'll take care of her."

"So she's okay?"

"See if you can stand up. Ready, set, go," and they lift him to his feet, supporting him on either side for a minute, and then they let him stand by himself. He wobbles a bit until he puts one foot out in front of him and finds his balance. He moves his arms about in a careful circle.

"So I'm not paralyzed?"

"Not this time," the younger one says.

"The news isn't *all* good, though," the older one says, but he is interrupted when the ambulance, lights whirling and siren screaming, pulls up behind the police car and slams to a stop with a long fine spray of sand. Renny and Toom hop out, all set for action. They take one look at Mandy and then they look at each other. "First time lucky," Renny says, "but not this time." "Aw, shit," Toom says, "aw, no! She was just a kid!" They examine her, determine for themselves that she is dead, and then check the time. Toom, upset, phones in the dead girl while Renny joins Jake and the cops, who are standing in a tight threesome.

"She's dead," Renny says.

"He doesn't know that yet," the younger cop says.

"He knows it now," the older one says.

Jake hangs his head and looks at the ground. He begins to shake, hard, but he makes no sound at all.

"You know what you are?" Renny says. "You are a dickless piece of shit."

†

The hospital has notified Rose and Dr. Forbes that there has been an accident, and later a Catholic nurse phones Father LeBlanc. Rose arrives first. She is nervous, uncomfortable, she doesn't know what to do. They show her to the room where Mandy's body lies and they leave her there, alone, for a short while. She does not pray. She gazes into Mandy's calm face, she smoothes her hair from her forehead, and then she lays the side of her face softly against Mandy's heart and listens to the silence there. "I love you, my baby," she whispers, "I'm sorry I failed you." But she does not pray and she does not ask the Virgin Mary for a miracle and she does not cry. She realizes now that for all these past weeks—ever since the miracle— she has been expecting this. Mandy was given back to her on loan only. At any minute her time might have been up, and now that minute has come. She wishes she had been a better mother, but it's too late for that. And still she does not cry.

Dr. Forbes enters the room carefully. He has had only a little to drink, but he is wary of Rose and Mandy and does not want to be caught out a second time treating the girl as if she's dead and having her wake up with nothing more than a headache.

"Rose," he says. "I'm very sorry for your trouble." He kisses Rose on the cheek and then leans over Mandy's body. She is cold, rigor mortis has begun to set in, and there is no doubt this time that she is dead. He is relieved in some way he can't understand, as if she should have been dead long before this. "I'm sorry for your bad trouble," he says to Rose. "I'll be just outside."

So she is alone with the body of her daughter, who has been dead once before and then came back to life and now is dead again. Rose does not understand it and she does not want to understand it. She wants it all undone. Her chest, inside, is hollow. A terrible light scours her brain, and her eyes feel as if they're bleeding. Again she lays her head on Mandy's heart, not praying, not hoping, only being with her daughter in death. A long time passes.

There is a commotion in the corridor, a man's voice, loud, protesting, and then a nurse calls out, and at once Father LeBlanc enters the room. "You can't go in there," the nurse says, "this is private," but Father LeBlanc closes the door behind him firmly.

Rose can see why the nurse didn't want him in the room. He looks crazy. His face is flushed, and his hands are shaking, and he is dressed in chinos and a windbreaker, not like a priest at all.

The nurse forces the door open, but Father LeBlanc, bent over Mandy's body, doesn't even notice. "It's all right," Rose says, "he's the priest." The nurse, still reluctant, goes away. Father LeBlanc has taken Mandy's pulse, at her wrist, at her neck, and now he has his ear to her chest, but there is no sign of life.

"This can't be," he says. "This simply cannot be."

"She's dead," Rose says.

"No. I refuse to believe that."

"She is."

Father LeBlanc looks at Rose carefully. How can she sit there, calm, tearless, and not see how wrong this is, how impossible? God performed a miracle and brought this girl back to life.

"Mandy is dead, Father."

"Then what was the point? Of the miracle?"

"Maybe she's been dead all this time and we didn't realize it," Rose says. She shrugs and places her hand over Mandy's. She bends down and kisses that hand. The skin is like stone.

"I'll never believe this," he says. "I'll never believe she's dead."

†

Father Moriarty is not surprised to hear that Mandy is dead. Almost nothing surprises him anymore. Nevertheless his tears start, because of Rose and then because of Mandy. And then just because we're all so easily broken and all so nearly good.

†

Father LeBlanc says the funeral mass and preaches a homily on the mysteries of God's will. We cannot understand mystery, he says, we must learn to live with it. Mandy was given to us for a short while and then taken away. What does her life mean? What does it mean for us? We can never know, except in its consequences: the good she has inspired, the love she gave and received, the memory she leaves, the promise, the hope. Mandy, in her too brief life, is an emblem of hope, he says.

†

Annaka Malley has returned from Boston to sell her parents' house and change her life forever. No more renting it out, much as she likes the extra money. No more high school English papers. Instead she's going to sell the damned house and go to law school. A year ago she was accepted at Suffolk Law but deferred entrance because of the cost, but now she has decided it's time: sell up and strike out fresh. She's going to be a lawyer. She's going to start a new life. Besides, she could never live in her parents' house. It would be like living her parents' lives, and that's one mistake she will never make.

At the real estate office, she hires an agent and agrees upon an asking price, which—even after the commission—will pay for all three years of law school. So it's settled, almost. Almost done. As Annaka is about to leave his office, the agent mentions the accident, the motorcycle death. Drugs, naturally. The girl, it turns out, was Rose's daughter.

And that is how their lives cross once again, and this time for good. Annaka Malley and Father LeBlanc. She attends the funeral mass and listens in disbelief as he speaks of memory and promise and hope. Mandy's life is an emblem of hope, he says. Is he crazy? The girl's future has been thrown away, trashed in some stupid motorcycle escapade: she has never lived at all. And yet this priest finds hope in it? He must be as desperate as he looks.

And then she's struck by something else about him. Father LeBlanc is handsome—yes, and he's sexy—and she knows that is part of what makes him attractive to her. But there is something irresistible about him that has nothing to do with his looks. He sees *beyond*. Whatever doubts he has, he's not caught up in the little things that wear her down, the loneliness and the isolation and the loss. He's above these things. He sees beyond them.

It comes to her quite simply: he is not of this world. He has given up this world and everything in it, comfort and vanity and even sex. She cannot begin to comprehend his life, but she can see that it is good. Her own life has been something else, one long pretense, but her ability to pretend has served her well. She has been an actress and she has tried stand-up comedy—twice, both times disastrous—and for the past six years she has taught high school English, pretending she knows how to teach, pretending she knows how to live. She has done what she wanted, always, and never given up a thing.

If she had courage, she could do it, too. Give it all up. Surrender? Surrender. She repeats the word over and over—surrender—and she begins to feel she might actually do it. But what about her life? What about law school? She looks at Father LeBlanc and she tries to pray. The mass ends, the coffin is carried from the church, everyone leaves. And still she sits there. An immense peace settles on her. She thinks she can almost see it, her future, her fate.

†

On the day after the burial, Monsignor Glynn makes one of his drop-in visits. Father Moriarty tells him about Mandy's death and the perhaps-miracle and then her death again, this time for keeps. Monsignor Glynn likes LeBlanc and wishes him well, so that afternoon he stops by the young priest's room to see how he's doing.

"You all right?" he asks.

"Aces," Father LeBlanc says. He puts down his book and gives Monsignor Glynn a thumbs-up.

"No, seriously."

"I can't talk about it now. Yet. It was a terrible thing."

Monsignor Glynn leans against the door frame. "Mind if I have a smoke?"

"Give up on the hard candies?"

Monsignor Glynn points a finger at him and shoots.

"Have a seat."

"No. I don't want to interrupt your work." He lights his cigarette and shakes the match but can find no place to put it. Father LeBlanc takes it from him and, instead of tossing it in the wastebasket, holds it up between his thumb and index finger, as if it were still hot.

"Death," Monsignor Glynn says. "It's a killer. Sorry, I didn't mean that the way it sounded. It's difficult. I think of Tom dying"— his eyes tear for a moment—"'We die, and we do not wish to die,' somebody said. What are you reading, anyhow?"

"A commentary on John. The raising of Lazarus."

Monsignor Glynn thinks how to begin, and after a while he says, "Let me tell you a little story. It's about Elizabeth Taylor and it's about death. Apparently she was making a film, *Butterfield 8* or something, and—"

"You're talking about Elizabeth Taylor the movie star?"

"Film actress, yes. She was making this film, and she got pneumonia and was dying, not a fake dying just for publicity but a real one, and she was in the hospital, and now that I think of it they even cut a hole in her throat, what do you call it, a tracheotomy, so it was the real thing, she was on the way out. Anyway, she was dying, she was a goner so far as anybody could tell, and it was in the newspaper and on television and everyplace, so everybody knew it and they were all waiting for the bell that tolls for thee, kiddo, and as she was lying there dying, she says she heard voices, thousands and thousands of voices, calling her, 'Elizabeth, Elizabeth, come back.' And she came back."

Father LeBlanc can't tell if this is some kind of sick joke or if Monsignor Glynn is serious. In any case, he lets out a burst of laughter. "What is this, comic relief?" he says.

"Seriously," Monsignor Glynn says. "I'm sure she thought it was a miracle."

Father LeBlanc is furious suddenly. "Jesus Christ," he says, "that's not funny!"

"Hey, sorry, sorry. I didn't mean to push a button here."

Father LeBlanc looks at him, still furious.

"I am sorry, really. Have dinner with me tonight and we'll talk. We should talk, Paul. About what happened with that girl. I wasn't making fun, honestly."

But Father LeBlanc stands up and says abruptly, "I'm due at the hospital." He throws the burnt match into the wastebasket.

"We can cook dinner," Monsignor Glynn says, and aims his finger at Father LeBlanc again. "Okay? I'll count on seeing you, Paul."

When Father LeBlanc returns from the hospital, he is no longer angry. Monsignor Glynn is a tough old bastard, but he's not deliberately mean, and Father LeBlanc is curious to know what he has to say. He is disappointed to find a note taped to his door, reading: "Called to Boston. Sorry. Trouble in paradise." It is signed, "Ed."

†

Father LeBlanc ascends the stairs to Rose's apartment and stands outside her door looking down over the harbor. It is the day after the burial, sunset, and the water glows orange and red and the horizon is a pale yellow line drawn against the sky. Father LeBlanc notices none of this. He has finally persuaded himself that Mandy is dead, this time for good. Rose has lost a daughter. He has merely lost a miracle.

He turns from the harbor, but before he can knock on the door, Rose opens it to him. She is not surprised to see him.

He goes inside and they stand for a moment facing each other, and then tears start in her eyes and she steps slowly, shyly, into his arms. He holds her stiffly as she cries against his chest. After a while she pulls away and says, "I'm sorry." She takes a tissue from her skirt pocket and wipes away the tears. "It's the first time," she says, and she realizes he does not understand. "It's the first time I've cried. I'll just wash my face," and she gestures him toward the living room.

Father LeBlanc stands at the window and thinks of the last time he was in this apartment: Mandy lay dead in her little bedroom, Sal and the doctor hovered around the bed, and Rose, pleading, drove them all out. Then there was that wild scream, death suspended, and Mandy came back to life. But now she is dead.

Rose returns to the living room.

"Okay?"

"I'm fine," she says. "I knew it had to happen again. And no miracle this time."

"It's hard to believe she's dead."

"I wish I'd done better. I wish I'd been nicer to her." The tears start again, but she brushes them away. "Can I get you something to drink?" she asks. "Some tea? Or a beer or wine?"

"And we're alive."

"Yes."

"A beer would be nice," he says.

Rose gets two beers and brings them into the living room, and then she goes back for the glasses. She pours his beer too fast and the glass overflows. This is more than she can stand, and she begins to cry again. He takes her in his arms.

"It's all right, Rose," he says, "it's just some beer on a table. It doesn't matter. It doesn't."

She begins to cry harder, she begins to give in to her grief, and it feels good not to be in control any longer, to let go, to let it all happen. She collapses against him, surrendering to the press of his body against her own. She wants to give in completely. She wants to hold him and touch him. She wants her mouth on his.

He pulls her closer and they fit together naturally, perfectly.

She feels she should keep on crying or else there's no justification for this, but she has cried herself out. She has no tears left.

She lightens the pressure of her arms about his waist, getting ready to stand back, to break away from the embrace, but he continues to hold her. She raises her head and looks at him. "It's all right," he says, and once more she buries her face against his chest and moves her hands on his back, slowly, like a lover. She is not thinking now; she is surrendering to the moment. It is getting dark outside and dark inside and she is very comfortable. She wants him inside her. She presses herself against him harder and feels an answering pressure.

Suddenly, sharply, he pulls away. It's as if he has been asleep and is now awake. "Rose," he says, "I'm sorry, no," and holds her at arm's length. "What am I doing?" he says. "I must've lost my mind. Here, come sit," and he leads her to a chair by the window and pulls up the matching chair close to hers. "You must forgive me, you have to forgive me, Rose, doing something like that, especially at a time like . . ." He stumbles, then stops. He assumes his priest voice then, and says, "I want you to know that I care."

"I know you do."

"So I apologize for what just happened here. I meant to console you, that's all."

"You did console me. You do."

"Let me do something for you, Rose. Let me get you something. Do you want that beer? Will that help? Here, drink some of this."

Rose sips the beer as if it is medicine and she is recovering from some kind of attack.

"Does that help?"

"It's good."

"Okay. All right." He stands up, eager to get away. "I'll come back some other time, Rose, when you're not so busy."

"I'm not busy."

"I mean when you've had time, you know, to recover, to get used to . . . the way things are now, with Mandy."

"All right."

"Well, I'll see you, then."

"All right."

Father LeBlanc backs out the door and disappears down the stairs.

Rose remains in the living room, looking out the window into the dark. She watches the schooner riding at anchor near the mouth of the harbor, its safety light brighter than all the rest, and she looks at the other, smaller boats with their lights. The black water and the lights, that's all there is. She thinks of Father LeBlanc again, and she feels his strong hard body against hers, and it is too much for her. She goes to her bedroom and lies down and thrusts her hands between her legs, pressing. She aches for him, she wants him. "God forgive me," she says, but she can't help herself. After a while the ache is satisfied, and she stretches out and buries her face in the pillow. She begins to cry, softly, carefully, ashamed for what she has done, and for what she has done to Mandy.

†

Father LeBlanc sits hunched over in the reclining chair beside Father Moriarty's bed and makes his confession. This is a LeBlanc that Father Moriarty has never seen before, humbled, shattered, because he held some girl in his arms and experienced lustful thoughts. Or at least he experienced an erection, and maybe lustful thoughts, too. He is deathly scrupulous about this recitation of sins.

Father Moriarty has never before heard his confession, and so he is not prepared for the idea of Father LeBlanc having lustful thoughts and he is not prepared for his scrupulosity. Though, thinking about it, scrupulosity fits perfectly with everything he knows about LeBlanc. Measuring progress, charting failures, working out some goddamn fiscal report on his spiritual investment: it's pitiful, it's sad. Actually, this momentary preoccupation with somebody else is the first sign of Christian life that Father Moriarty has seen in the boy. Poor kid. Poor shit.

If only he could think of something helpful, but all he can think to say is: Stop, you're not that important, not your sins and not even your virtues. And that doesn't seem very helpful at the moment.

"You feel very bad about this," Father Moriarty says.

"I've failed, badly."

"Failed yourself? Or the girl?"

Father LeBlanc is shocked. "I've failed God."

"Of course," Father Moriarty says. "But God's perfection doesn't depend on yours, does it, so the failure matters less to him than to you." He pauses, but LeBlanc says nothing. "God uses our failures, sometimes, to remind us that we're merely human. This might be the best thing that could happen to you . . . stop trying to strong-arm God into making you a saint."

Father LeBlanc remains silent.

"God doesn't *need* our goodness."

"But *we* need it."

Father Moriarty is about to say, *Not as much as you think and not as much as you'd like.* Instead he says, "Hmm."

He tells Father LeBlanc to say three Hail Marys and make an act of contrition. Then he recites the Latin formula for absolution, and insofar as he physically can, he makes the sign of the cross over Father LeBlanc's bowed head and smiles—kindly, he hopes—into the near distance.

†

It is deep night and the ocean breeze has moved ashore, bringing with it the smell of the ocean and the sour grasses that grow along Church Lane. There are funny noises all around the place: floorboards that creak for no reason, the on-and-off hum of the refrigerator, and outside and down the path there is the continual croaking of frogs. They keep at it. They never seem to tire. Glub, glub-uh-glup. Father Moriarty listens to them croak and he thinks how all things living praise the living God. If there is a God.

He has lived his life in fear, but now, when he should be most afraid—the angel of death is crooning right behind his pillow—he is not afraid of anything. How do you explain that? He is not even afraid there may be no God after all. Maybe there are just lots of little gods. Little terror gods that tick off the moments of each life, push us into easy, cowardly decisions, warn us not to say too much, do too much, love too much, because it will all be taken away one day, and meanwhile we should live a measured life, a restrained life, a selfless life. Or God will get you.

Maybe LeBlanc is right, and you've got to be miserable to become a saint. Maybe saints like him are called from all eternity. "Yoo-hoo! It's God calling, sweetie pie, and have I got a surprise for you." He says this aloud, in the voice of a Jewish mother, and it pleases him, so he says it again. "Yoo-hoo, *bubelah*! Come give us a hug! Surprise! Surprise!" He wishes he could do accents like Eddie Glynn. "Ve have vays to make you talk!"

He thanks God for leaving him his voice till the last. What a lucky bastard he is!

†

And across the corridor Father LeBlanc has flung himself across his bed and prays to be forgiven. Then he prays that he has not done Rose any permanent damage. And while he prays, he thinks, Yes, but one touch is enough to bring the city crashing down. He wants to know her. He wants to possess her.

He is not attracted to her in any way, but he must possess that miracle.

Suddenly he is aware he is not praying, and he prays to be allowed to pray without temptation, without distraction. He prays to leave her alone, to never again sin with his hands or his arms or—he is erect again, despairing—any part of him whatsoever.

Make me like Father Moriarty, he thinks, make me motionless, emotionless, a sack of bones thrown into a bed, incapable of sins of the flesh. It's an easy prayer and he knows it, because God never offers you sanctity on your own terms. He always comes up with something unexpected.

Somewhere far down the beach, a dog barks halfheartedly and then stops. There is silence.

†

And across the corridor Father Moriarty listens to the silence and says, "Sleep, oh blessed sleep," and he is happy, as if it all means something, as if it all has some purpose, as if there is a God.

†

And across the corridor Father LeBlanc gets up, strips to his underwear, and gets back into bed. Forgive me, dear God, he means to say, but instead he says, "Rose, forgive me," and then he sleeps.

The frogs continue to croak through the night, glorying among the lily pads.

†

A new day, dawn, a new beginning.

Father LeBlanc has gone running, he has made his meditation, and now he is saying mass. He is very tired. He was awake much of the night, and he is distracted by the problem of Rose: how to face her this morning, how to face her every morning hereafter? Rose is honest and frank. He is not. She will not forget their embrace and she will not pretend to, whereas he wants yesterday evening forgotten; he wants it never to have been. He prays for guidance.

And so when Annaka Malley comes into the sacristy after mass, Father LeBlanc is elated to see her. She looks beautiful, untroubled, and that makes him happy. Also, he'll have another chance to talk with her instead of preaching at her like the last time they met. And best of all, he now has a reason to skip breakfast in the kitchen with Rose.

"Welcome!" he says. "Welcome back!" and Annaka seems pleased at the unexpected warmth and enthusiasm. "How are you? I've missed seeing you. I was afraid that I talked you to death last time and I'd never see you again. What a pleasure!"

"It's clear to me now, I think, what I was looking for."

"Good, oh good, we must talk about it," he says. "Let me finish up here and then I'll see you in the parlor. All right? We can have a talk. We can have a good talk."

"I'll only need a minute," she says.

"I've got plenty of time," he says.

"I hate that parlor." She adds, by way of apology, "I'd rather tell you here. I'm selling up, the house, I mean, and I'm thinking of entering the convent. If they'll have me."

He stares at her, stunned.

"I just wanted you to know."

There's a loud rap against the open door. Father LeBlanc turns and sees it is that idiot, Jake, who has been showing up everywhere since the accident. He waves the boy away.

Annaka says, "I thought you might like to know, since it's partly because of you."

"Please," Father LeBlanc says. "Wait. We have to talk about this. You can't—"

Jake raps again and says, "'Scuse me?"

"Thank you, Father." Annaka smiles, radiantly, and leaves the sacristy. She passes Jake with a little nod, genuflects toward the altar, and is gone.

"Excuse me?" Jake says, knocking yet again.

Father LeBlanc looks at him, hard.

"Can I talk to you, Father?"

Father LeBlanc swallows whatever he was about to say and says instead, "You can see me at ten in the rectory parlor, Jake. And whatever it is you've got to say, it better be good."

"I can't go in there, man," Jake says. "*She's* there."

"Rose, you mean."

"Jeez," Jake says.

"Tough, isn't it, to face up to what you've done?"

Jake nods. "I can't go in there."

"I know." He would like to tell Jake to go to hell. Where he belongs.

"So, can I, like, talk to you?"

Defeated, Father LeBlanc picks up the metal folding chair from beside the sink and places it opposite the only other chair in the room, the one by the prie-dieu. "Have a seat, Jake," he says. "And talk."

Jake is not used to talking except in short phrases, and he has never talked to a priest, so this is not easy. "It's like it's not real, man," he begins, and after a long while Father LeBlanc comes to understand that Jake feels responsible for Mandy's death—"But not really, man, not like I did it on purpose or anything"—and he would like to do something to make up for it. He has been off drugs for four days now. He can barely stand it.

"You want me to tell you what to do?"

Jake nods, rubs the fuzz that's beginning to show on his shaved head, and he tugs at his nose ring.

"What do you *think* you should do?"

"Hey, man," Jake says, and spreads his hands, palms up, meaning, *How am I supposed to know that?*

"Well, you can start by staying dry. Right?"

"For how long?"

"Jake." Father LeBlanc shakes his head. "Have you tried a twelve-step program? You've got to try a program, A.A. or something. You can't do it on your own. You know that."

"Well, I don't *want* to do it, like, forever. I just want to do it till I make up for what I did, like, with Mandy."

Father LeBlanc leans forward, earnest, determined. "Listen to me. The first thing you've got to do is get dry and stay dry. That's the best thing you can do for Mandy. It's the best thing you can do for Rose."

"I am dry. That's what I'm telling you."

"For four days."

"Right," Jake says, proud of it. "Four freaking days!"

"Okay, good, very good. So you're dry for four days, and they're probably the hardest, so you're doing very well. Very, very well. But you've got to get help, don't you see? Otherwise you're gonna get tired or depressed or worried and you're gonna go right back to the stuff, you know that, and it's only a matter of time till you're on that goddamn bike, stoked to the gills with coke or pot or heroin, and you kill yourself. You know that. You must. Now look, there are A.A. meetings at Cobb Point every day. There's even a meeting, once a week, maybe twice, at the Vets Hospital. You could go to that. You could stop in and take a look. See that it's not threatening. It's a help. It is. There are good people there." He waits a moment. "Jake? Are you listening?"

"You're not very practical," Jake says. "I want to *do* something."

"God help me," Father LeBlanc says, half to himself, half to Jake.

"Thanks anyway," Jake says, and gets up. He pauses at the sacristy door and looks back, as if he has one more thing to say. But then he shrugs, raises his hand in a wave, and leaves the church.

Father LeBlanc continues to sit there, looking at the swirl pattern in the green linoleum, wondering what he could have said, what he could have done. Because he knows, he is certain, that Jake is doomed.

He starts to hum "Cry Me a River" until he realizes what he is doing and then stops at once.

†

Mrs. Schwartz has bathed Father Moriarty and given him clean sheets and a glass of iced tea. She settles down for a little chat with him.

"Well, now," she says. "What have you been up to?"

He gives her a look. "Rose's daughter died," he says.

"I know. Drugs and motorcycles. It always ends like that. They should abolish them."

"Yes," he says.

"Still, I feel bad for the mother."

"Yes," he says. "Rose is wonderful."

"And I feel bad for the other father." She gestures toward the corridor.

"Father LeBlanc? Why do you feel bad for him?"

"I just do," she says. "It's as if he died, too. Take a good look at him."

Father Moriarty nods and she nods and that marks the end of their little chat.

†

A week has passed since Mandy's burial, and Father LeBlanc can think only of Rose. How awful this must be for her: a motorcycle hits a patch of sand and her daughter breaks her neck and dies. It's incomprehensible.

He forces himself to think of Mandy. He never knew her, really, never paid attention to her, not even after she was restored to life. What he remembers about Mandy is that she was a little sexpot, a temptation to all the horny young guys who hang around Salisbury Beach waiting to get lucky. But that's not fair. For all he knows, she might have been a very nice young girl, a little bit wild maybe, the way you should be as a teenager, but a good and loving girl with a fine future as a devoted wife and mother. Is there anybody who still thinks that's a fine future? Is it? Mandy, at any rate, will never have any future, fine or not fine.

Rose. Rose is alone, in what loneliness and despair he cannot imagine. He could comfort her. He should comfort her.

He has kept away from Rose ever since that evening at her apartment when consolation almost led to mortal sin. All this week he has managed to avoid having breakfast in the kitchen; each morning he comes up with a new excuse. He has seen her at mass and he has seen her taking care of Father Moriarty, but he has not allowed himself to be alone with her. Rose has been the victim of a miracle gone wrong. He will not further complicate her life by making her the victim of his lust. Is it lust to want to understand a miracle?

The sun is about to set as Father LeBlanc climbs the stairs to Rose's apartment. Again he stands and looks out over the harbor.

The last rays of sun dazzle on the water, and as he watches the waves glitter and go dull, he becomes aware of a tiny flame flickering in the corner of his eye. He watches the water and the flame, waits for the black butterflies to make their descent, the sense of motion inside his head, his brain shifting, the muffled thrashing of wings and the singing. He waits, and it happens as it has before, and in another moment his vision clears. He shakes his head once, takes a deep breath, and knocks on her door.

She opens to him and they make love.

# SIX

IT IS DARK NIGHT WHEN FATHER LEBLANC KISSES
Rose softly on the mouth and says good-bye. He casts a quick glance
over the harbor—nobody's around, there are no lights anywhere—
and he goes quietly down the stairs and around the front of the Clam
Box. His is the only car in the parking lot. He unlocks the door,
opens it, and stands there looking up at the black sky.

He is exultant, he can't help it, he feels alive in a way he has
never been before. He stretches. He puts his hand to his crotch and
it feels good. He has a soul and a body, and for the first time in his
life he's made complete use of this body. He has made love to another
person. It's terrific! It's great!

It is mortal sin, of course . . . he knows that . . . but is it really?
How could it be sin, something as natural and inevitable as this.

He has completely forgotten about his need to comprehend
the miracle.

He breathes the wet air deeply, and he feels good, he feels wonderful. He feels Rose opening to him once again, and his naive,
unused body, hard and right, responding to hers. They move in
unison. They thrust. They ache. Finally they come together and
dissolve in each other's arms. It is a kind of worship. What can possibly be wrong with that? Even while doing it, he had thought, This
is not sin, this is what the body is made for.

"Thank you," he says to the night air, grateful to be alive, a man, a lover.

He gets in the car and drives slowly north to Church Lane and home. Only yesterday he was wallowing in despair, and today, tonight, he is a different person. A little nervous, a little anxious, but a new person. He thinks of Rose lying in bed, alone now, and he knows she is glad, satisfied, even though she is going to be upset tomorrow because she has had sex with a priest. She will be worried, confused. That's the worst part of what he has done. It was sin from the moment he took her in his arms, not only this time but the earlier time as well. He thinks back to that other night. He had just buried Mandy, and it was only the girl's death, he supposes, that kept them from falling into bed right away. They waited a week. Or rather he waited a week. She would have waited forever. So he is to blame.

I am to blame.

I am to blame.

He is home now. He has parked his car in the church lot and is sitting there, looking up at the empty sky. I am to blame.

This is certainly not what Father Moriarty had in mind when he said, Try loving somebody besides yourself just for once.

He gets out of the car and goes into the house. He is thirsty. He's dehydrated from all that thrashing around in bed, so he stops in the kitchen for a drink of water. No, he will not drink anything. Not until tomorrow, after he has gone to confession. At least make that little offering to God, for Rose's sake, a prayer that she won't be permanently damaged by what he has done. He's like one of those priests you read about in the newspaper, molesting altar boys, stealing parish money. The only difference is he hasn't been caught yet. But of course he's exaggerating. He hasn't taken up fucking as a way of life; he's fallen once. He mustn't exaggerate this. He takes a sip of water. What presumption to think that not drinking water could make up for what he's done. He downs the whole glass and pours himself another.

"Fucking takes it out of you," he says aloud, and shakes his head in disgust.

He goes slowly up the stairs and into his room. He sits at his desk—he can't bring himself to the hypocrisy of kneeling—and says, "Our Father, who art in heaven," but the words go dry on his tongue. It's hopeless, he can't pray, he can't even kneel. He gets up and begins to pace the room. "I'll wait until tomorrow. I'll wake Father Moriarty early and he'll hear my confession. And then I'll go on normally." He paces some more. And then, as if it happens without his consent, he leaves his room and goes to Father Moriarty's room and hunches over in the reclining chair by the bed.

"Father," he whispers, and gives the bed a little shake.

Father Moriarty's eyes open a crack.

"You've got to hear my confession," Father LeBlanc says. "Father?"

"What's wrong?" Father Moriarty is still half asleep, still half in his dream of a baseball game. He was pitching, and there were two outs and he was winding up, splendidly, for the next pitch, a strike. "What?" he says again, a little annoyed.

"I slept with a woman," Father LeBlanc says. "I had sex with her."

Father Moriarty tries to sit up in bed, but of course he cannot, and his hands fumble on the sheets and his head jerks from side to side.

"What time is it?" he says.

"You've got to hear my confession, Father. Please." And he launches in, his voice quavering, "Bless me, Father, for I have sinned . . ."

Father Moriarty is awake now. "Father, Father, please," he says, exasperated, "this isn't penitence, it's panic. It's hysteria. Give me that water, would you?"

Father LeBlanc holds the glass to his lips and he drinks a little. "Now what the hell are you talking about?" he says.

"I've got to confess, Father."

"Now? In the middle of the night?"

"I've committed fornication, Father. I don't want to go to bed with a mortal sin on my soul."

"Never mind your own soul for once. Think of the other person. Think about the woman. Does she have some priest she can wake up in the middle of the night to confess to? What about her soul?"

Father LeBlanc bites his lip and says nothing.

"You're not penitent, anyhow. You're just panicky. You just want to square the deal with God."

Father LeBlanc stops then and thinks. Father Moriarty is right. He is panicked, that's all. An hour ago he was covered in sweat, pleased with himself, the stud. And twenty minutes ago he was standing in the Clam Box parking lot, looking at the sky, and asking, *How can it be wrong and why*. And now he is covered in guilt, he's rolling in it—a pig in shit, he thinks—pleased to condemn himself to hell if that will mean it's all over. But it's not all over. It will never be all over.

"Do you hear what I'm saying?"

"Think about the woman, you said."

"Yes, do that. Think. Then wake me in the morning and I'll hear your confession. All right? *Don't* give way to melodrama, Father. God is still on your side."

"If there is a God," Father LeBlanc says.

"And don't be a smart-ass, either. Wake me in the morning. Before mass."

Father LeBlanc goes back to his room.

†

Rose kissed him good-bye softly and stood at the door watching him go down the stairs. Now she stands looking out over the harbor. It is dark out there, not a light, and the water looks like velvet. She listens for the sound of his car starting up, she thinks she hears it, and she goes back to bed. She is relaxed, she stretches full-length in her bed, her legs wide open to receive him, and she moans with pleasure. Then she curls up, her knees at her chest, and she sighs. She has wanted this forever, it seems, and now she has it. Tomorrow she will have to pretend it never happened and make sure it never happens again, but that's tomorrow, and tonight she can still dream about him, feel his hands all over her body, give herself to him in her mind again and again. She sleeps, gladly, and dreams of making love to him.

In the morning she wakes, kneels beside her bed to ask forgiveness, and inhales the smell of their sex on the sheets. There is no hope of praying here. She strips the bed methodically, stuffing the sheets inside the pillowcase, and then she makes the bed up fresh. She plugs in the coffeepot. She leans on the windowsill overlooking the harbor and confides in the Virgin. "So this is me now, seducing priests, and what can be left that's worse?" She waits for an answer and is relieved when she doesn't get one. "Okay," she says. She promises she will go to Cobb Point on Saturday and confess her sins, and she will never sin with him again, that beautiful priest, the most beautiful man she has ever seen, and she will reform her life, amen.

But what if it should happen again? She hopes it will. She can't help it.

She has sinned against Mandy and against the priest and against the Virgin. She only hopes she will live until confession on Saturday, not that she believes in hell, but just the same . . .

Meanwhile she has a nice cup of coffee.

†

Father LeBlanc has made his confession very early this morning. Father Moriarty listened patiently, kindly, and then surprised him by asking how he felt. Guilty, he said. As well you might, Father Moriarty said, but don't exaggerate the importance of what you've done. You're not the world's greatest sinner, you're merely another in a long line of sinners. But the woman, Father LeBlanc asked, what should I do about the woman? Tell her you're sorry, Father Moriarty said, if you think you're sorry, and don't disturb her any further. Don't be alone with her and don't talk with her about it, because talk will become reminiscence and reminiscence will find you in bed again. Got that?

Father LeBlanc thinks about this during mass and during his thanksgiving and he is thinking of it now, still, as he sits eating his breakfast.

It is less than eight hours since they have made love.

He forces himself to swallow a bite of toast. He does not know what to expect from Rose. She is silent, but what does that mean? Silence can turn to hysteria in ten seconds. What if she decides that last night was the beginning of a long affair and she starts in with little touches, little gestures of ownership? Or what if she is furious? His mouth is so dry that every moment he feels he will choke.

She pours him more coffee and takes the pot back to the stove, and then he says it.

"Rose?" It is almost a whisper.

She turns and looks at him.

"Are you all right?"

"I'm all right," she says. "I'm sorry."

"*I'm* sorry," he says. "I went to confession before I said mass. I wouldn't want you to think—"

"No," she says.

"It's a sin, Rose. I can't . . . I shouldn't have . . . it's my fault."

It seems wrong to eat anything more, and God knows he is not hungry, so he sits, looking at his folded hands. Rose goes over to the sink and stands, looking into it. After a long while she turns to him and asks, "More coffee?" and when Father LeBlanc shakes his head, she says, "I'll go dust then."

"I'm sorry," he says again.

"Don't be," she says.

And that is the end, he hopes, of what has happened between them.

†

Father Moriarty lies in bed thinking. They are two lovely people, LeBlanc and Rose, and what a nice couple they would make. Because it must be Rose he's been to bed with. Who else could it be? LeBlanc is impossible, of course, with his sanctity shtick and that fascist spirituality he practices. What woman could put up with him? Whereas Rose is easy, uncomplicated. But still, it would be nice if they had met and married and had kids, like normal people. The last temptation of Christ: to normality? They could have made love till they were blue in the face.

Father Moriarty shrugs, or tries to. He himself has never made love. And never will. Not ever.

"Sing hi, sing ho, sing hey nonny-nonny."

His voice floats out into the corridor, and Father LeBlanc, on his way up from his talk with Rose, hears Father Moriarty singing and wonders what kind of spiritual life this man must have. He shakes his head. It is not for him, the worst of sinners, to judge.

†

A week has passed with everything quiet. Rose, having confessed her sins on Saturday in Cobb Point, comes dutifully to work and does her job and goes home. Father LeBlanc is back on his schedule of praying and running and official visits: to the Veterans Hospital, to County General Hospital, and to the Portsmouth prison, where he teaches a Thursday-evening class in remedial English. And Little League on Wednesdays and Saturdays. And his own nightly study of Scripture. The parish accounts. Letters to and from the bishop.

Everything, apparently, is back to normal, except that he skips breakfast and goes to any length to avoid seeing Rose. Inside, however, Father LeBlanc feels he is coming apart. He reminds himself, in the voice of Father Moriarty, that he must not give way to melodrama, that panic is not penitence, and *don't* talk about it. But he is not Father Moriarty. He is just a poor dumb priest who aspired to sanctity and offered to cut a deal with God and failed at it, within minutes, it seems to him now. "Love me," he had said, "and do with me what you will." Ha!

Sometimes at prayer he is overwhelmed by temptation. The feel of her skin, the raw force of her pelvis against his, the soft sleek flesh of her inner thigh. But this is only lust, and he does not confuse it with love. The sad truth is that he has injured her and now, guilty, wants nothing to do with her.

He prays, and runs, and works, but he knows that if God were to show up in the sacristy after mass tomorrow morning, he would not have the courage to look at him. "Help me," he prays, "dear God, send me help."

The next morning it is not God but Annaka Malley who shows up in the sacristy after mass.

†

Father Moriarty has a numb feeling in his throat. He lies in bed and sings out, "Ro-oh-oh-se," and his voice sounds to him as loud as ever, but he doesn't feel much of anything back there in his throat. He feels his tongue, he thinks, and he clicks it against his teeth, and he chews on his lower lip and he feels that, too, but there is definitely a difference. The good old ALS is moving in and taking over. One by one the muscles give up. Pretty soon he'll lose the ability to speak and then the ability to eat—they'll insert a feeding tube down by his stomach somewhere—and finally he won't even be able to swallow his own saliva. He'll be dripping here and there, all over the place. Nice.

He remembers his mother's death and knows his own won't be any prettier. "Grow old along with me, the best is yet to be," he recites, thinking, You can be sure whoever wrote that was some asshole who was thirty years old. Browning, most likely.

At the end, even the eyelids will give up; he'll be effectively blind unless somebody tapes them open for a few minutes at a time, the way they did for his mother. Will he see differently in the near light of eternity, if there is eternity? We don't change much, even when we want to; we simply become more of what we are. And after the eyelids shut down? It could be days. It could be years. He'll just have to wait and see . . . or not see, as the case may be.

"Ro-oh-oh-se," he calls out. "Where is my goddamn breakfast?"

†

It is two weeks since Annaka Malley told him she was entering a convent and had come to say good-bye. He had been grim then, appalled, and she was disappointed. Before he could smooth over his reaction and blame it on surprise, that idiot Jake showed up, twitching and scuffing, and she went away with everything unsaid. Now they are standing in the church parking lot, uncomfortable with each other, but Father LeBlanc can see she is very happy.

He is determined this time to be supportive, upbeat. He will be glad for her. He will be joyful. He has failed her before as he has failed everybody—*Rose, Rose, Rose, forgive me*—but now he is being offered one more chance.

"Welcome," he says. "Welcome back!"

"I've come back to sell the house," she says. "I may have a buyer."

"Come into the rectory and tell me. I want to hear all about it."

"I hate the rectory," she says. "That parlor, I mean."

"I know. It's . . . dead." He looks around the gravel parking lot and suddenly says, "Wait. I'll change my clothes and we'll go out to breakfast. I want to hear all about it."

He goes into the rectory by the side door and waves hello to Rose. When she calls out, "I've made toast," he pretends not to hear her and disappears up the stairs. Even he has to wonder: what is he up to now? He has been cold to Annaka Malley—Annaka, he thinks, what an awful name—and then he has spilled out his most private life to her, with his problems of faith and hope and despair, and now he has invited her to breakfast. He has spoken to her no more than three or four times, he has kept her distant, and now he finds he is excited to see her. Thrilled. He must be crazy. Well, he *is* crazy, everybody knows that, and she's off to the convent pretty soon, and the least he can do is buy her breakfast. He changes out of his clerical black, and in less than a minute he comes thundering down the stairs in chinos, a Red Sox T-shirt, and his beat-up sneakers. He sprints across the parking lot and gets into Annaka's little green Mustang—"Aw-right!" he says— and they drive away. They head north along the coast.

"So tell me," he says, and for no reason, he laughs.

"About the house?"

"About the convent."

She laughs, too. He is in such a good mood, and the day is gorgeous, and the convent doesn't matter anymore.

"Do you ever just want to sing?" he says.

"Singing is my life."

"Singing is my soul." He tosses back his head and becomes Ethel Merman belting out "There's no business like show business."

By the third line his voice goes flat and they laugh together as if this is a terrific joke. Annaka lowers the register and sings the line on key.

"Easy for you to say," he says.

"Well, it's wonderful," she says.

"What is?"

"Life. Just living."

"Tell me about the convent. What order, by the way?"

"Oh," she says. "Sisters of Notre Dame. But that's a thing of the past, I'm afraid."

He looks at her. A question.

"They told me to forget it. They said, 'Take two aspirins and it'll pass.'"

"You're joking."

"Actually, they were nicer than that."

"But they said no?"

"Anyhow, I'm selling the house and going to law school. I'm going to get a law degree. I'm very excited about it."

"Wait, wait, wait," he says. "Two weeks ago you're entering a convent. Now you're going to law school? How is this possible?"

"It's easy for me. I'm a complex and fascinating woman." She shoots him a wry look, half mocking.

He begins to sing again but goes flat at once.

"What they said was this: I should think some more about it, and if I'm still convinced I have a vocation, I should come back in a year. Meanwhile, I shouldn't give up my day job."

"Seriously, though."

"I am serious. I'm always serious. I think I just wanted . . ." Her voice trails off, and she lifts her hand from the steering wheel as if she is tossing something away.

"Wanted?"

"You know."

"I don't know."

"To be you."

He has been watching her closely and sees she is serious. He puts his hands to his neck and pretends to strangle himself.

They are smiling, nervously.

"Turn in here," he says. "It's a truck stop. They always serve great breakfasts."

†

Rose spoons cereal into Father Moriarty's mouth, and he seems to swallow it, but then it comes out again.

"I'm not hungry," he says.

"You're never hungry. You've got to eat and keep your strength up."

"It's too late. I'm all done," he says.

"Don't say that. Please don't say that."

"I meant I'm all done *eating*. Jeez!"

Rose sits beside the bed, thinking. She cannot tell him about Father LeBlanc. After a long while, she speaks.

"My Mandy was dead and then she came back to life."

"Yes."

"It was a miracle."

"Yes."

"And then she died."

They are silent for a while. They are both thinking of Father LeBlanc.

"God works in strange ways," Father Moriarty says.

"I feel like I should feel sorry . . . for some things I've done. But I don't feel sorry."

"No."

"Do you think I should feel sorry? For some things?"

"I think we all should feel sorry. For everything."

She lowers her brow until it touches his, and they remain this way for a moment. This poor man. This poor dying man, she thinks.

Once again she does not say she is in love with Father LeBlanc.

†

Annaka Malley and Father LeBlanc eat breakfast slowly. She has coffee and a corn muffin, and she makes it last the whole time he is eating his two eggs over-easy, bacon, toast, and a cup of diced fruit. He works his way through it methodically, as if it is a duty, and then he pushes the plate away.

"I ate too much," he says. "I hate myself when I do things like this."

"Like what? Eating breakfast?"

In fact, he doesn't know why he said it or what he meant by it, so he changes the subject. "Tell me about your family. Rose says your father died a couple years ago?"

"Yes," she says. "He killed himself. Hanged himself." He looks pained for her, but before he can say anything, she rushes on. "Tell me about the priesthood. How did you happen to become a priest? Well, I guess 'happen' isn't the right word."

"In a way, it is. It happened to me. One day I was talking with my college roommate, who always liked to goad me, you know, pick my brains apart, and he was good at it, he was very smart, he was a debater. He had always wanted to be a doctor, and he was on his way to being one, he was really smart, and I wanted to be an actor or a writer or something."

She interrupts and says, "An actor?" but he continues on.

"And he said to me, 'That's all frivolous, Paul. What you ought to do is enter the priesthood. I'll tell you why. It's the best thing anybody can do with his life'—from the point of view of eternity, he meant—'and there are no moral impediments to your doing it, apart from being a little crazy, which is not really a moral impediment when you consider who all are priests, and there are no intellectual impediments, because you're smart enough. So. You can and you should, therefore you must.' And I said that applied as well to him, so why didn't he enter the priesthood himself and leave me out of it. And he said because he was called to be a doctor and always had been. 'Whereas you,' he said, 'aren't called to be anything, you've admitted it yourself, so you *should* be a priest.' That's how it happened."

"Oh." She sounds disappointed.

"That's how it happened," he says.

"You're that easily convinced?"

"I wasn't convinced by *him,* by what he said. It's just that God uses people in this way. He meddles in our lives. You don't have to be a prophet to deliver a message."

"So," she says. She is relieved when the waitress interrupts to pour them more coffee. The waitress goes, finally, and Annaka says, "Have you ever been tempted *not* to? Be a priest?"

"Usually twice a day, first thing in the morning, last thing at night. Sometimes more often."

"But you stayed. You stay."

"Yes."

"Do you think I'm being a little too blithe, then, in forgetting about the convent?"

"No, no. They don't want you. Case closed." He sees her flinch and says, "It's the old message theory. Sometimes God says no. I mean, maybe the convent saying no is God's way of telling you to be a law-yer. Though it's hard to imagine he wants more lawyers in this world."

"Very funny."

"No, I think you should do with your life what *you* want to do. Life is short, mean, and brutish and you shouldn't waste it doing the, quote, best thing you can do with your life, end quote, just because people say you should. You know?"

"But isn't that exactly what you did? Isn't that what you just said?"

"It's something I *want* to do."

"What do you mean by *want*?"

For a long time the word hangs, unexamined, in the air. And then he says, "I warn you. I'll sing again. And this time it'll be "Born to be Wild.""

Annaka has no choice but to laugh. He laughs, too, and then he pays the bill and they leave.

†

Father LeBlanc has changed Father Moriarty's sheets and put clean pajamas on him and lingers now by his bedside.

"Thank you," Father Moriarty says, and closes his eyes, exhausted.

"Can I ask you something?"

"You mop up my shit, you make my bed, you give me clean pajamas. What more could you ask?"

"I want to ask you about being a priest."

"Oh Christ," Father Moriarty says.

"No, I have to ask you this." For a while Father LeBlanc says nothing. "I became a priest because I thought it was the best thing I could do with my life, and since I *could* do it, I *should* do it, and so I did."

"I know that."

"How could you know that? I didn't know it until today."

"You told me."

"No."

"In those very words."

Father LeBlanc sits, silent, thinking. "Huh," he says, "okay." He continues to sit there, but after a while he gets to his feet and goes away. In a few minutes he comes back.

"Well, what do you think of that? Becoming a priest because you can and therefore should."

"The issue is what do *you* think of it."

A long silence.

"Well, it wasn't that I wanted to be a priest. It was that I wanted to sacrifice . . . my life."

"You wanted to be a saint. That's what you want."

"No, I wanted to give my life to God."

"You wanted his approval. You wanted the heavens to open and a voice to appear, saying, 'This is my beloved son, in whom I am well pleased.'"

"A voice to *appear*?"

"Logic chopping won't change the facts."

Father LeBlanc withdraws into himself. He has to find the right words. He feels that his whole life, his priesthood, is at stake. Finally he says, "But God—"

"Doesn't need you. Doesn't need me."

"But he loves—"

"To see you suffer?"

Father LeBlanc looks down at his folded hands. He thinks, You don't have to be a prophet to deliver a message. "Do you want some water?"

"I want some Scotch," Father Moriarty says.

"You want, you want," Father LeBlanc says. "What do you mean by *want*?"

†

Rose prays to the Virgin every night and every morning, asking her to take away the feelings of lust for Father LeBlanc. It will require, she knows, another miracle, but she does not doubt that it will be granted someday. Meanwhile she offers her sufferings—that thorn in the flesh, the hollow ache that starts between her legs—for the repose of the soul of her daughter, Mandy, who was taken away from her and given back for a month and then taken away forever, amen.

In confession this afternoon, the priest at Cobb Point told her she must quit her job and cease to be an occasion of sin. She has never thought of herself as an occasion of sin. She isn't. She couldn't be. Father LeBlanc, however, is an occasion of sin for her—she'd like, God forgive her, to crush him between her legs and never let him loose—so maybe she should quit her job after all. "Mary help me," she says.

†

Yesterday Annaka Malley and Father LeBlanc went out to breakfast, and today, Sunday, they are driving north to Portsmouth for breakfast once again. They talk about old films and old Broadway musicals, and he tells her about his family: his father a lawyer, his mother a grammar school teacher, his twin brother dead, drowned on a school picnic, tragic, a waste. She tells him about her two years as an actress—she skips the stand-up comedy disaster—and what it's like teaching high school now that the Vietnam War is over, and together they've reached that comfortable moment when a little silence between them feels companionable.

"What kind of name is Annaka?" he asks.

"Why, do you hate it?"

"I love it. It's just . . . unusual."

She laughs because she knows he hates it. "It's really Anna Kathryn," she says. "I just shortened it for theater."

From now on when he thinks of her, it will be as Anna Kathryn.

"That's nice," he says. "You're nice."

The mood in the car changes.

"I like knowing you," she says.

"You don't know me at all," he says.

But I'd like to, she thinks. And you'd like me to. And, she thinks, I could love you back to life.

"I'm up here as punishment," he says. "They wanted me out of Boston."

So, he likes to talk about himself. He is like other men, after all.

"Tell me," she says.

"I was trouble. In my parish, St. Matthew's, I was against the war, and I said mass in English before it was allowed officially, and in confession I wasn't tough enough on crime."

"On crime?"

"You know, the Roman Catholic notion of crime: masturbation, premarital sex, birth control."

She's not going to touch this. She'll let him get around to it himself.

"Not that I was trouble, really. I was perfectly orthodox, more or less." He waits for her to smile and then he goes on. "I mean, I didn't say, 'Way to go!' when they confessed these things, but I'd play down the importance of them, and sometimes, with birth control, I'd say straight out, 'Why do you consider this a sin?' And I'd help them form their conscience."

"So you *were* trouble."

A smile plays at the corners of his mouth.

"And pleased about it."

He makes the gesture of pulling a knife out from between his ribs.

"Well, aren't you?"

"I'm guilty of spiritual pride, is what you're saying."

She laughs, and he tries to laugh, but it doesn't work. The laugh goes sour, and he says, "In fact, I'm a fornicator. Not as a regular thing, I mean, but I'm guilty nonetheless. There's not a lot of room left for spiritual pride."

She nods her head in agreement but does not look at him.

"Guilty as sin," he says.

"But not as a regular thing."

"No, but you are what you are. I am this . . . failed . . ."

"But you'd be the first to say that God forgives sin, especially that kind of sin."

"But I'm a priest."

"He doesn't forgive priests?"

"He doesn't forgive me."

"But that must be heresy," she says. "Why should he forgive other people but not you?"

"Well, he does, actually, but—"

"But *you* don't forgive you, is that what you mean?"

"Yes."

He looks at her, hoping she will understand.

"Then you're right," she says. "I don't know you at all."

†

Even though it is still baseball season, two kids in the church parking lot are tossing up a basketball. When they see Father LeBlanc
come out of the rectory, one of them says, "Hey," and the other
one echoes him, "Hey," and Father LeBlanc responds, "How ya
doing?" They start playing rough to impress him, and one of them
says, "Shit," but not too loud. Just as Father LeBlanc reaches his car,
the ball goes out of bounds and he stops it with his foot. He bends
down, bounces it twice, hard, and then a third time, and then he
leaps high, the ball rises gracefully from his right hand, arcing through
the air for thirty feet or more, and—chunk—it swishes through the
net without even touching the rim. "Yes!" Father LeBlanc says, and
slides into his car. "Aw-right!" the kids shout.

It's going to be that kind of day.

He is driving to the Veterans Hospital and he feels good.
"You'd be the first to say that God forgives sin," she said, "especially that kind of sin." She's right, of course. He would say that,
he says it all the time in confession. Back when he was studying
canon law, he decided that the problem with the Church is that
very early in its history it got into the sex business. This is wrong,
this is right, this is a mortal sin, this is a venial sin—unless there's
malice of intention and then it's a mortal sin—the primary purpose of sex, the secondary purpose of sex: who could have dreamed
it all up? *Adulteria perfecta et completa,* for instance, as opposed to
mere *adulteria perfecta*. It's insane. When he gets to the Vets Hospi-

tal, he's gonna preach a homily on mercy and justice. No, he'll preach on mercy only; they've all seen enough justice. Stop worrying about sin, he'll tell them, stop worrying about what God thinks of you, God thinks you're just fine. And for God's sake, forget about guilt, guilt is paralyzing, guilt is death.

And he does this. He says the noon mass and he preaches his homily. The doctor and the two nurses and the ten veterans who attend mass listen to Father LeBlanc and think how good it is to hear a homily like this, how nice it is to have a priest who's on their side, how handsome he is, how smart he is, how happy he is in his vocation.

After mass he makes his thanksgiving and is surprised to see Jake waiting at the door of the chapel.

"Man," Jake says, shaking his head, "man, I can't tell you, no shit!"

"Jake," Father LeBlanc says, surprised, since he's never seen the boy at mass before.

"Man, if I could only believe that, like, forgiveness and all like you said, because I am really freaked about Mandy. Like I don't know what to do, man."

"Yes, well. Why don't we talk about it?"

"I know, I know, you want me to clean up my act. But I'm clean, man, two weeks almost. Come on! Nothing! Just a little weed."

"Good for you, Jake," Father LeBlanc says.

"But I really need to know when my time is up, man, with being off drugs and all. I mean, like, I can't keep dry forever. I'm like really strung out!"

"Just for today. And then tomorrow. One day at a time."

"Yeah, like I don't see through that? Ha! I wasn't born yesterday. I'm a thinking person, too, you know."

Father LeBlanc can't help smiling.

"Sure, make jokes," Jake says, and slouches away.

Father LeBlanc watches him go. "See ya, Jake," he says, and sets off to the wards to visit the sick, though for the most part they are less sick than traumatized. There are amputees and there are blind men and there are many who seem to have nothing wrong with them. These are the most serious cases. With the druggies, he listens, since there's nothing else he can do for them. He talks to the ones who want to talk, and if they don't want to talk, he sits beside them for a while and says something dumb like "How you doing?" until they respond to him or turn away. He is good at making conversation about nothing. He even seems to enjoy it. Later in the afternoon he writes a letter for a kid who has lost his right hand and refuses to learn to use his left. He talks with the nurses and the doctors. He talks with the visitors. He talks with the staff and the building custodians, and he would like to talk to Jake. Father LeBlanc is young and alive and—he can hear them thinking it—a really nice guy.

It's been a long day but a good one. He's done something for people. He's made them conscious of God's mercy. His joy. His love.

He drives home trying to think about what a good day it was, but the day is behind him now, and all he can think of is his own particular sin, his own ineradicable guilt. Why can't he offer himself the comforts he offers to other sinners, to any sinner, no matter how far gone? But he doesn't. He can't. And he does not know why, except that he seems to have chosen this living death.

†

Father LeBlanc is dreaming of Rose. He has entered her, and as she clutches his back, he thrusts and keeps on thrusting, but he cannot

JOHN L'HEUREUX

come. "I love you, I love you," she whispers. "Wait!" he says. "Wait just a second," and he grinds his teeth, gasping, and at last he comes. He kisses her softly on the mouth, and as he does, the face beneath him changes and he sees it is not Rose he is kissing but Anna Kathryn Malley. "No!" he says, horrified, and thrusts her away from him. He wakes with no memory of the dream but he is cross and sweaty. He has a headache that lasts the entire day.

†

Annaka Malley does not understand Father LeBlanc, but why should she? She has never understood men at all. She has lived with three of them, and loved them for a while, but as soon as marriage was an issue, she moved out, away, preferring silence with herself to the silence of marriage. She would never marry. She would have married Devin—at the end when he was dying—but by then the cancer had done its job, and his lungs gave out, and he died breathless, choking. She loved him, dying, and loved him more when he was dead. He was safe then.

She shakes her head. She's the classic case. She has spent years with a shrink, and she understands. This is her parents' house, where they lived out their terrible married life, silent, furious, needing each other's anger to go on. She has inherited their house and—despite the shrink or because of him—she has inherited their lives as well. She will sell the house, leave it, and start a new life, this time for real.

She puts on her bathing suit and lies on the back patio in the sun. It's a perfect day, clear with a soft breeze, and even though you can't hear the waves this far from the beach, you can feel the salt sting in the air. She could love this house if only . . . but there is always an if only, and she is determined now to live in the real world. Father LeBlanc.

Her first love affair was with Jackson, an actor ten years her senior, who taught her whatever she knows about craft. "We're alive onstage," he'd always say. "Only onstage. It doesn't matter what your life has been up until now; it's all useful, no matter how terrible it was; it's all just stuff we use to create an illusion onstage. It's the illusion that's real. The rest of it is make-believe." She liked this, living for the two hours when you create an effect on the stage. You moved people. You made them feel. What *she* felt, of course, was irrelevant. Which was nice, since what she most wanted was to feel nothing at all. She spent two years with Jackson and then he asked her to marry him—she had great gifts, he said—and immediately the affair was over.

Henry was a mistake from the beginning, tall and sexy, a stockbroker in love with romance. He wanted candles at dinner, and good wine, and he liked to get up in the middle of dinner and say, "I need you, now," and take her off to the bedroom to make love. Even at the start she found this ridiculous. By the end of a month she was bored with him, and by the end of two he was bored with her. The breakup was painless. He was on to someone else before she had even packed and left.

And then Devin.

And now? It is all a snare and a delusion. Who said that? She must ask Father LeBlanc. Perhaps he knows.

Annaka Malley applies sunscreen, postponing life for a little while.

A cloud drifts across the sun, and for that moment there is a chill in the air. She puts on her dark glasses so that when the sun comes out again, it is no more than a dull red disc in the sky.

†

The morning is blessedly cool when Dr. Forbes makes his weekly visit to see how Father Moriarty is doing. Actually, he has not visited in more than a month, but he means to visit more often, and Father Moriarty is willing to pretend that he does, so when Dr. Forbes asks how he is doing this week, he says, "Fine, just fine."

"And it's a fine morning too. Nice and cool," Dr. Forbes says.

He listens to Father Moriarty's heart and takes his pulse and blood pressure and nods knowingly.

"So I'm still alive?" Father Moriarty asks.

"Pretty much," Dr. Forbes says, "though the lungs seem weaker." He taps them and listens carefully. "Yes, I'd say they're definitely weaker." He says this as if it is something Father Moriarty might be pleased to hear.

"Well, I'm working at it," Father Moriarty says.

"You might take a glass of wine now and then. Isn't it Saint Paul who says to Timothy, 'Take a little wine for thy stomach's sake'? Something like that?"

"Look at me," Father Moriarty says.

"I'm looking."

"No, I mean look here, right at me."

Dr. Forbes shifts his eyes up so that they meet Father Moriarty's. He looks away quickly and then he looks back.

"About how much longer?" Father Moriarty says.

"Oh, that's hard to say."

"How much longer?"

"Weeks? Maybe a month, or even two? I'm only a doctor, I'm not God."

"Alas," Father Moriarty says.

# THE MIRACLE

†

They are walking, silent, the long length of the shore. It is a rocky beach at the northern end of the coastline, and very few tourists come here even in high summer. Today is cloudy and the beach is deserted.

Father LeBlanc and Annaka Malley walk side by side like an old married couple. He twirls a thin stalk of eelgrass between his fingers, rolling it back and forth, beginning to shred it. She walks with her fingers twined behind her back, her head tilted up.

He glances over at her and sees that she is far away, thinking.

He is thinking, too, and he would like to talk to her about it, but of course he cannot. He is thinking of his guilt. He is thinking of Rose. He has slept with her, he has made love to her, but he does not love Rose. He was obsessed and, in his stupid-ass way, trying to get at the miracle . . . which had nothing to do with him. He knows that. Since then he has kept clear of Rose. He skips breakfast. He keeps away from the kitchen. They both know it was a mistake, and he has made his peace with her. If only he didn't have to see her at all. Ever. And he thinks, It is true, we come to hate the innocent we injure.

He is suddenly cold, empty. He looks over at Annaka, who is still gazing up at the sky.

They walk to the edge of the headland, where there is an old wooden bench. They sit and look out over the water.

Really, *this* is what life should be, he thinks: sitting beside someone you like, looking out over the water, not even thinking.

They sit for almost an hour, and then they walk back to her car and she drives him home to the rectory. He goes up to his room, where he flops on his bed and thanks God for . . . he can't think for what, exactly, so he thanks him for everything.

†

Monsignor Glynn enters the bedroom and tries to conceal his shock at how awful Father Moriarty looks. The dying priest is little more than bones. "How are you doing?" Monsignor Glynn asks, and as if reading his mind, Father Moriarty recites:

> *I'm death upon wires*
> *And bones in a sack,*
> *Poverty riding*
> *On misery's back.*

Monsignor Glynn chooses to take this as a joke. "Sure, and you're looking grand," he says, slipping into an Irish accent.

Father Moriarty is delighted. "That's what me old grandmum used to say when you asked her how she was. She was from County Armagh—up north, 'where we fight for our faith,' God help her—and she had these wonderful Irish expressions. 'Have you seen Mary Claire Doherty now? A lovely girl, she is, but beef to the heels like a Mullingar heifer.'" He laughs softly. "What else? 'Did you try some of your aunt Sarah's own bread? Tough stuff it is, 'twould knock down Mike Kelly's wall.' 'And what are you doctorin' for now? Keep away from those medical men. They'll kill you, you know.'" And, exhausted from this burst of entertainment, Father Moriarty turns his head on the pillow and falls asleep.

Monsignor Glynn watches for a while to make sure Father Moriarty is sleeping and not dead. He opens his breviary then and reads Psalm 137, the song of exile:

# THE MIRACLE

*By the waters of Babylon,*
*There we sat down and wept*
*When we remembered Zion.*
*On the willows there*
*We hung up our lyres.*

It's a psalm he always turns to, he allows himself to think, when the shit gets too thick on the ground. There is nothing sad about the psalm—it's a consolation—and there is nothing really sad about Tom Moriarty. He is dying, that's all. At last he'll be free.

Almost at once there is stomping on the stairs, and Father LeBlanc taps on the open door. "Just wanted to see how Father is doing," he says.

Monsignor Glynn nods and points at Father Moriarty, asleep.

"Sleeping?" Father LeBlanc says.

Monsignor Glynn nods again.

Father LeBlanc catches on finally and lowers his voice. "How about dinner? Tonight?"

Monsignor Glynn nods twice.

"You're on." Father LeBlanc stops whispering and points his finger at Monsignor Glynn and shoots. He thunders down the hall to his own room.

Father Moriarty smiles and opens one eye. "He's being thoughtful," he says, "by whispering."

"He's a mess," Monsignor Glynn says. "He's an unreconstructed mess." And then he smiles because there is something awfully winning about the boy.

At seven, dressed in their clerical suits, Monsignor Glynn and Father LeBlanc drive off to dinner. They discuss where they'll go and what they'll eat, and they end up going where all the locals go, to the Sandpiper, for fried clams and french fries and apple pie. Father LeBlanc orders a Scotch and Monsignor Glynn orders a double Scotch and they fall into conversation like old friends.

"So how's it going? The exile."

Father LeBlanc laughs out loud.

"Are you converting Tom?" Monsignor Glynn is enjoying this. "To your way of thinking?"

"You should worry that he's converting me. 'Thank God, if there is a God,' he always says."

"That doesn't mean anything. He's always been like that. He's very saintly, is Tom."

"Well, he suffers, that's for sure."

"Nobody gets out alive," Monsignor Glynn says.

Father LeBlanc hesitates, but this is the chance he's been waiting for—"Nobody gets out alive"—and he plunges ahead. "Did Father Moriarty ever tell you about the miracle? About Rose's daughter, I mean, dying?"

"You tell me. I'm all ears."

"She died. She overdosed on something, some drug, and by the time Rose got to her, she was dead. There were witnesses." He tells Monsignor Glynn about Dr. Forbes and Sal and Jake, and about Mandy coming back to life, and then the motorcycle accident and Mandy's death, again, finally.

"That's it?"

"That's it."

"Well, I should imagine she wasn't dead, that's all, it was just a . . ."

"Just a miracle."

"Why call it a miracle? Why not call it a wonderful thing? Is she up for canonization or something?"

There is a silence between them, and then Father LeBlanc says it. "I slept with her."

Monsignor Glynn shakes his head.

"It wasn't what you think—it wasn't only sex—it was because I was trying to get to the miracle."

"Or trying to get into the sack."

"You think I'm kidding myself," Father LeBlanc says, and at the same time Monsignor Glynn says, "Sounds to me like you're kidding yourself."

"No, you've got it wrong. It was a sin. I'm not saying it wasn't. And I've confessed it. And kept away from her. I haven't been alone with her once since it happened."

"Lower your voice."

"But that's not why I'm telling you."

"Why *are* you telling me?"

The words come to him, and he tries to choke them back, but they come out anyway. "Maybe because I want you to tell me to stop being a priest."

Monsignor Glynn puts his finger inside his Roman collar. He is sweating.

"Is that what you want? To stop being a priest?"

"Well, I've come a long way from wanting to be a saint, haven't I. I guess the next step—"

Monsignor Glynn sees what is happening and begins to talk fast. "We all want to be saints," he says. "You can be a saint without being a priest, that's for sure. And look at us, we're proof that you can be a priest without being a saint. You know, people always say they want to do the will of God, and they wonder what it is, when it's just a matter of taking what's thrown your way. ALS for Tom, I suppose. And this job of mine for me. For you? Maybe living with who you are."

"And who is that?"

"Aha! That's for me to know and you to find out. Or vice versa. Whichever applies."

They laugh at this, like two men engaged in a common search. They order their apple pie with a little vanilla ice cream.

"Did you ever see *The Wicker Man*?" Monsignor Glynn asks. "Edward Woodward. Now, there's a film actor."

†

It is late August. The weather remains beautiful, only now the long hot days are interrupted by a cool afternoon breeze. The light on the ocean seems softer, making the water a silver gray. It will be fall soon.

Father LeBlanc and Annaka Malley are at the beach—their beach, they call it—the long rocky stretch of coast, and she has brought a picnic basket and he has brought champagne. He thrusts the bottle into a red plastic bucketful of ice while she spreads a beach blanket on a little patch of sand. She unpacks the goodies—fried chicken in a box and some French bread, a block of Swiss cheese, a carton of strawberries—and they sit down at opposite sides of the blanket and pick at the food. Then they lie back and gaze out at the water.

He glances over at her. She is wearing sneakers and white pants and a blue-and-white-striped boating shirt. Her blond hair is streaked with pale yellow. She looks very young to have lived with three different men and left them all. She has told him about them. She keeps nothing back. For a moment he is jealous of Devin, dead of lung cancer, who knew her in a way he never will. There is a whole world in her that he will never know. He is jealous of Devin. And a little hurt.

"Tell me about Devin," he says.

She tells him everything she has told him before.

"You really loved him," he says.

"One another," she says.

"Tell me about Jackson," he says. He wants to know her. He wants to touch her.

"Tell me about God," she says.

He looks startled, as if she has said something she has no right to say. She reaches out to touch him but stops herself. He is a priest. A little crazy, a little mixed up, but nonetheless a priest. She pulls back her hand. "It's time to go," she says, and they gather up the blanket and the picnic things. They haven't touched the champagne.

†

They walk barefoot along the beach, their beach, and the waves break on the shore, sending the salt spray up around their ankles. Sandpipers scurry around them, seagulls glide and swoop in the distance. The sun is pale on their backs.

Annaka Malley understands she could seduce him. She is in love with him. He is handsome, and he has that body, and she feels bad that he has a kind of self-loathing that is almost pathological. He needs to be held and touched. He needs to be consoled. A picture flashes before her eyes: she lies down on the beach and takes him inside herself, deeply, till he touches her heart and is made whole at last, and he smiles, he laughs out loud. She blinks the

177

picture away. Seducing is one thing. Seducing a priest is another. No. It's not for her.

At this moment Father LeBlanc takes her hand in his, lightly, and swings their arms back and forth as they walk. Like kids on the way to school. Like pals. Like lovers?

†

Rose cleans the rectory, saying her Hail Marys the whole while, and she puts a six-pack of chocolate-flavored Ensure in the refrigerator, and now she goes upstairs to check on Father Moriarty. She has to talk with him today, no matter how hard it is.

"I'm going now," she says, "unless I can get you anything?"

He shakes his head.

"I can stay for a minute or two if you're a little bit lonely."

He can see she wants to talk. "Talk to me," he says.

She searches for a way to begin. "Father LeBlanc is at the Vets Hospital today," she says. "It's Thursday, is why. He works really hard." Father Moriarty says nothing, so she goes on. "The attendance at mass is falling off the closer we get to Labor Day. And it's not so sunny, of course, that has something to do with it." She cannot bring herself to say she is in love with Father LeBlanc. Mercifully, the doorbell rings. "I'll be right back," she says.

It is that woman, Annaka Malley, at the door. She wears no hat today and her face is drawn, but as always she looks cool and elegant. She smiles and says hello. Rose returns the smile and says, "Father LeBlanc isn't here," but her voice is even colder than she intended, so she adds, "He's at the Veterans Hospital. It's Thursday."

"I was sorry to hear about your daughter," Annaka says, and goes on to offer those consolations—so young, so tragic, so terrible a thing—that mean nothing at all. "I wish there were something I could say. There *is* nothing anyone can say, is there."

"No," Rose says. "But I'll tell Father LeBlanc you called."

"Actually, it's Father Moriarty I'd like to speak with," Annaka says. "I know he's very ill, but—"

"Father Moriarty doesn't see people." Rose lowers her voice to a whisper. "He's dying."

"I know. I need to speak to him."

"Well, I don't know."

"Could you ask him? For just a few minutes? We're old . . . well . . . friends. He knew my father and mother. He buried my father. Tell him Malley? Anna Kathryn Malley? Maybe he'll remember."

Rose opens the door wide and leads Annaka into the parlor.

Upstairs Rose explains to Father Moriarty. "This is a woman who comes to church all the time. She's a close friend of Father LeBlanc." She waits. "It's too much for you," she says. "You're not strong enough for this." She waits some more. "She's from around here, I guess, originally. Her father committed suicide. Anna Kathryn Malley."

Rose shows her up to the room.

"This is Father Moriarty," Rose says. "Don't make him too tired."

It is more than a sickroom, it is a tomb. Annaka can feel death in the air. She can smell it.

"Anna," Father Moriarty says, smiling.

"Anna Kathryn," she says. "You were very kind to my father."

He nods, yes, he remembers.

She looks around the room at all the equipment needed for

dying and thinks of Devin. "I shouldn't be bothering you," she says, "now."

"Nevertheless," he says.

She sits in the chair by his bed and tries to state her problem succinctly, but what comes out is a jumble: her father's suicide, the death of Devin, Father LeBlanc, the breakfasts at the truck stop, the picnics, the walks, the talks and the silence. And then, finally, she gets to the point. She is in love with Father LeBlanc.

"I love him," she says.

"Why?" he asks.

Is he joking?

"I mean, why? How? Do you even know him?"

The walks, the picnics, the silences.

"Well, you can't," he says. "You mustn't."

"I know."

"Then why are you here?"

"I can't help myself. I don't want to. It's like a . . ."

"A compulsion?"

"I was going to say like a call from God."

"Some call," he says. "Some God."

He counsels her then on what she must do and what she must not do. In short, she must pray for guidance and strength, and she must leave Father LeBlanc alone. He says exactly what she expected to hear, so why did she bother?

She is about to leave when he asks her if Father LeBlanc knows she is in love with him.

"We've never talked about it."

"Don't."

She lingers at the door.

Father Moriarty prays for guidance: *Give me one thing to say, now if never again,* but nothing comes to him.

"My father killed himself," Annaka says, "because he couldn't live without my mother. He needed her to hate."

"If in doubt, choose life," Father Moriarty says, whatever the hell that's supposed to mean.

†

Rose is jealous and ashamed of it. But she can't help being jealous of Annaka Malley, with her beautiful clothes and her thin body and her ability to charm. First Father LeBlanc and now even Father Moriarty.

She drives home thinking of this woman, nearly her own age, and she wonders why some people get born rich and beautiful and others are like herself. It's not fair, but then nothing about life is fair. She has always known that. It's just the way things are.

Like losing Mandy, and getting her back, and losing her forever.

She wishes she wouldn't, but she can't help thinking of Father LeBlanc's body, hard and muscled and all over her, his hands on her breasts and down there, too. She wonders if Annaka Malley knows what this is like. She hopes not. She wants Father LeBlanc for herself, she wants him to stay a priest and never have sex with anybody else, she wants to be the only woman he ever has.

"I'm a whore," she says aloud. It's fucking that she loves, not Father LeBlanc. "God forgive me," she says. She parks the car outside the hardware shop and goes inside. She'll buy something, anything, miniblinds, maybe. And she'll say hello to Nick.

Nick Pappas waves at her from the back of the store and comes out to greet her. "Looking good, Rose," he says.

She smiles at him. He's fifty-five, at least, but he's a sexy devil, tall and lean.

"What can I get for you? You name it. We got it."

What she wants is exactly this, flirtation and excitement and then a long night of sex. But it is not even noon.

"Miniblinds," she says. "I need miniblinds for my kitchen."

"We've got 'em, lots of colors, lots of sizes. What size do you want?"

"I don't have a measuring stick. Do you suppose you could do it for me? Measure?"

"No problem, Rose. Glad to. I could come over to your place anytime. Right now, if you want. Or later tonight."

"Come at nine," she says. "I work till nine at the Clam Box."

That night Nick Pappas measures her kitchen window for miniblinds, after which they have a glass of wine and sit looking out at the stars, and eventually they go to bed. For this while, at least, Rose gets Father LeBlanc out of her mind.

†

Jake has been hanging around the church after mass, and on Thursdays he listens carefully to Father LeBlanc's homilies at the Veterans Hospital, and he is now convinced that Father LeBlanc is useless. Only Rose can forgive him.

He goes to the Clam Box during her evening shift and sits at the corner table with his cup of coffee, waiting for the moment when they'll be completely alone in the shop. But it never comes. Sal wanders in and out of the back room. That retard Luis keeps showing up to mop the tables even when they don't need it. And the local kids come in and push one another around and spill ketchup and vinegar and turn the place into a regular shit house. They have no respect for anything. Jake goes outside and sits on his motorcycle, waiting for the place to close down.

A little after nine Rose comes out and goes around the building and up the stairs to her apartment.

"Aw-right!" Jake says, and gives her a minute to settle down and then follows her up the stairs.

He knocks at the door and waits. He looks out over the harbor and sees that, even when you're not high on drugs, it's a real pretty sight. He's still admiring the lights on the boats and the stars in the black sky when the door opens and he hears Rose gasp.

"You!" she says.

This throws him off, but only for a second. "Rose," he says, "I want to apologize from the bottom of my heart and I want to ask you to forgive me."

She looks at him as if he is crazy, and her face begins to contort with rage.

"I really mean it. I need you to forgive me," he says.

She begins to slap at his face, and when he puts up his hands to protect himself, she goes at him, wildly at first, and then with determination. She wants to hit him hard, she wants to hurt him. She punches his chest and his arms, and when he crouches over, she pummels his shoulders. He steps away from her, backward, and his foot slips on the landing and he is thrown off balance. He tries to straighten up, and as he does so, she shoves him, hard, and he tumbles facefirst down the stairs, slamming against the railings as he falls, and landing with a terrible dead sound at the bottom. He lies there silent for a moment until he feels he can move. He gets himself into a kneeling position and then he stands up slowly, painfully, and looks up the stairs at her.

"You're crazy," he says. "Jesus Christ, you're crazy."

Rose looks down at him for a moment, relieved that he is still alive, and then she goes inside and slams the door.

†

Father Moriarty lies with his eyes closed because he is more comfortable that way. He is not sleeping, he is resting his eyes, but then he feels himself beaten about the face and head, punched in the chest and pummeled on the shoulders, and pushed finally down a long flight of stairs. His back feels broken and he is sure his legs won't work, but somehow he manages to get to his knees and then to his feet. It is only when he begins to walk away that his eyes fly open and he realizes he must have been asleep after all. But why does he ache all over, and why does he have this lump on his head? He closes his eyes once more, but this time he is careful not to fall asleep.

†

Father LeBlanc has said mass. He is kneeling in the sacristy, making his thanksgiving, but all he can think of is Anna Kathryn Malley. She has left the beach and gone back to Boston without a word. Well, actually, she stopped in after Sunday mass to say good-bye, but there were people around and it was a formal good-bye and she might as well have left without a word. Something has happened between them and he doesn't know what. He misses her.

Last night he dreamed of making love to her. The dream began with Rose; he was consoling her, "It's all right," he said, "it's all right," and he embraced her, slowly, and they sank onto the bed and suddenly it *was* all right, and they were free, and as he entered her and bent his face to hers, she said, "Love *me, love* me," and it was not Rose at all but Anna Kathryn, and he said, "Yes," and "yes." He woke up happy and excited. He misses her. He sees her face, her hair, those gray eyes, and he realizes he has an erection. At prayer, no less. Is this the new Paul LeBlanc, stiff as a poker, moving from woman to woman? He has not finished being guilty about Rose and he's moved on to Anna Kathryn? Way to go! *Quel* stud! He is disgusted with himself.

Suddenly he thinks, But I love her, as if he knows what that means.

He shakes his head to clear it, makes the sign of the cross, and returns to the rectory. He opens the door softly and starts upstairs, but Rose comes out of the kitchen and says, "Father?" And so he's trapped.

Father LeBlanc and Rose have coffee in the kitchen, or rather she serves him coffee and then busies herself wiping at the counter, which is already clean.

"I was wondering when I'd see you again," she says.

"I know."

"I miss seeing you."

"We can't," he says. "And I've been busy."

"But you see that Malley, that Annaka Malley."

He lowers his eyes. He lowers his head.

"I'm sorry," she says.

"*I'm* sorry."

He sits, waiting for more. This is the easy part of the punishment because it comes from the outside. What's really hard are the dreams and the distractions at prayer and the constant guilt.

"I can't," he says again.

"We could at least walk together. You used to walk me home."

Nothing.

"Come on. You can't deny that," she says. "It was nice.There's nothing wrong with just walking together." Then she says, "It's not like walking is a sin."

He looks up and sees a new Rose. She wants to punish him, and God knows she has reason enough. So he's guilty of that, too, making her vindictive.

"Father Moriarty isn't doing so well," she says.

"It can't be much longer, Rose. It's good that he'll die at home. With the people who love him."

"Everybody loves Father Moriarty." She stands at the kitchen counter thinking, and then she says, "I have to talk with him about . . . things," and goes upstairs.

Father LeBlanc knows what she will talk about with Father Moriarty. Well, more punishment. More justice. He finishes his coffee and rinses the cup and puts it in the dishwasher.

He is alone with himself and God. This is what he signed on for.

†

Rose has been with Father Moriarty for a long time now. He lies there with his eyes closed, listening. She feels bad telling him that she slept with a priest, because he'll probably guess it was Father LeBlanc, but it will serve him right. He used her for sex and now he's neglecting her.

As she makes her confession, though, something unexpected happens. She finds she *is* sorry for what she has done. She didn't really feel sorry before. In fact, she wanted it to happen again and soon. That's why she's mad at Father LeBlanc, because he doesn't want it. So she confesses this also. And as soon as she does, she is surprised to find that she feels bad for him. And for Father Moriarty, too, having to listen to all this shit. She is moved nearly to tears. She feels so bad that she tells him about her sins with Nick Pappas and with the others she has picked up in Salisbury, even though it makes her sound like a whore. Whatever she is, she's sorry for it, and she tells him everything.

"I've sinned a lot," she says.

Father Moriarty says nothing, but he shifts his hand so that he can pat her wrist.

"I need you to tell me what to do."

"Just try, Rose," he says. "You're a good woman. You don't want to cause people grief, isn't that right?"

"But what do I do about Father LeBlanc?"

"Rose." It's an admonition. She should not have used his name.

"He doesn't love me."

"What *can* you do?" He speaks very slowly and with effort. "That priest, whoever he may be, is a priest. He can't stop being a priest, and you can't—you must not—make it more difficult for him. He's working out his salvation in his own peculiar way. If you love him, you won't interfere."

"Yes?"

He falls silent and remains silent. She waits.

"What else?" she asks.

"That's it."

"The other priest, in Cobb Point, told me I should leave here, I should quit my job, and not be an occasion of sin."

"Yes. You can't let yourself be an occasion of sin."

"But I don't want to leave you until you're . . . you know. And I don't think I'm an occasion of sin."

"No," he says. "Yes."

"I think *she* is. Or was."

"Rose," he says.

"I don't know what to do." She takes his hand in hers and squeezes it. "What would you do?"

"Let him go," he says.

She does not reply.

"Will you do that?"

Still no reply.

"Will you? For me?"

"Yes."

Father Moriarty is out of breath. He can barely speak. "Let him go," he says one last time, and then he gives her absolution.

That night she is so lonely she can't bear it. As soon as she gets off work in the Clam Box, she makes herself a gin and tonic, just for company. And when Nick Pappas shows up with flowers and a bottle of wine, she invites him in, and inevitably, they drink and fool around a little and then go to bed. This isn't what Father Moriarty had in mind, but it's the best she can do.

†

Since the beginning of September, Annaka Malley has been living in Boston, studying law at Suffolk University. She has not yet sold the beach house her father left her, so she comes back on weekends and works around the place. September is not a good month for unloading beach property.

She goes to mass and she sees Father LeBlanc, but she does not see him afterward in the sacristy. She is keeping her distance—thanks to Father Moriarty—and she knows she should keep away from LeBlanc altogether, but she loves him and she needs to see him, so what can she do?

They do not go out to breakfast and they do not walk on the beach. They do not even talk together.

Father LeBlanc is drifting. He has begun to teach his night class once again, he is busy with his hospital visits and his visits to the prison, he performs all his priestly tasks dutifully and well. Sometimes he phones Anna Kathryn in Boston and sometimes here at the beach, but she never answers and never returns his calls. He does not know why she has moved out of his life. He misses her. He wants her.

†

Father Moriarty is slipping away, and even he has begun to notice. His speech is halting now, and when he tries to sing—just for the hell of it—his voice comes out in a sort of croak. It's funny, and he likes to hear the sound, but it's exhausting, so mostly he lies quietly with his eyes shut, holding a good thought for Father LeBlanc and Rose and Annaka Malley. Is this prayer? he wonders. And if it is, to whom am I praying?

†

Jake is mopping the corridor at the Vets Hospital, and he has paused to gaze through the glass door of the pharmacy. It's locked, of course, and even if it wasn't, all the really good stuff is double-locked inside the metal cabinets—which seems to him to indicate a lack of trust in the employees. Anyway, he's not interested in the pharmacy, because he doesn't do drugs these days. He could use an upper and a couple downers, that's for sure, but he's not going to touch anything anymore. You have to get through today, that's what they all say, one day at a time. He's got grass, and that helps, but it really isn't the whole answer. Grass, jeez. But no drugs *today*. And—but they don't want you to think about this—no drugs tomorrow or the next day or the rest of your freaking life. Why keep on living if you can never have drugs at all? What are you supposed to do with your time? He turns back to the corridor and mops it with new vigor and determination. No drugs today or tomorrow or ever. Yeah, sure. Easy for you to say.

†

Father LeBlanc is thrilled because Anna Kathryn has phoned and made a picnic date for Saturday. He knows why she has disappeared from his life—he has been indiscreet and she feels threatened—and he is elated that she is willing to come back. This time he will be very careful. No talk of leaving the priesthood. No touches. No intimacy of any sort. He is willing to sacrifice love if he can keep her friendship, which after all is better than nothing. He vows he will choke before he'll let himself use the word "love" with her.

Annaka Malley drives up from Boston with a picnic basket full of treats. There is *pâte de campagne* and shrimp and cold chicken. Brie and French bread. Blackberries. Sparkling apple juice. Real plates and real glasses.

She has decided the time has come to find out where they stand. She has even prepared a speech she will deliver when the time is right. It's not complete, but in one of its many forms, it goes like this: "When I was a girl, my mother and father refused to speak to each other except through me, so every day was a new discovery of what it meant to be truly alone. And bitter. I blamed marriage, of course. I determined I would never marry. Even when I fell in love, I knew I couldn't marry, not even Devin when he was dying. And then I met you, and it was like a revelation. I knew the first time I saw you that you were the one man I could marry. But you are a priest . . ." This is as far as she gets in her speech, because at this point he will have to say something himself—about leaving the priesthood or not wanting to leave the priesthood—but *something*. She can't be the only one willing to . . . what? . . . propose?

She deliberately arrives too late for mass so she won't have to see him in his vestments. She swings by around ten and picks him up in the parking lot beside the rectory. They drive north—no singing today—and they make oddly formal conversation on the way to their beach. They talk about the weather: she is wearing jeans and a heavy sweater and has brought a jacket as well. They talk about law school. They talk about the horror stories coming out of Vietnam, now that the U.S. is out of the war and the Vietcong have taken over the south. By the time they get to their beach, she has begun to question the wisdom of her plans—what if he's shocked, what if he's insulted?—and she decides at least for now to leave the picnic basket in the car. "The breeze is really cold," she says. "Maybe we should take a walk instead."

They walk along the rocky shore until they reach a patch of hard sand, and then they walk more slowly, side by side. He picks up a bluish shell. She picks up a stone. Neither says anything.

In her mind, she rehearses: I determined I would never marry. Even when I fell in love, I knew I couldn't marry. And then I met you, Paul. She will say it.

They stand looking out to sea where a ship appears, riding the horizon, and they watch it move slowly across their line of sight until it disappears altogether. It takes a long time.

"Paul," she says, and then she hesitates.

He waits. He will keep on waiting no matter how long it takes. He won't mention the word love, in any context, at all, ever . . . unless she mentions it first. Instantly his heart tightens. He has one of those strange, inexplicable intuitions: she is going to say she loves me. If she does, if she even hints at it, I'll tell her I love her. I'm leaving the priesthood. And will she marry me? He waits, and he waits, and when he can't stand it a second longer, to keep from saying I love you, he says, "Look at this shell. Have you ever seen a blue shell like this?" He holds it out to her.

There is a silence.

This was the moment, but the moment had passed. It's impossible now. She had been ready at that exact second to say I love you, but now it's too late.

"That's a fairly common shell, actually," she says. "It's a mussel, or a kind of mussel anyway," and they talk about shells and the color of shells and the shells you might find along this beach.

"It's getting cold," she says at last. "We ought to turn back."

He is depressed, he walks with his head bent, and they are silent as they return to the car. He puts his arm loosely about her shoulder, but she shrugs it off. They drive in silence all the way home. As she lets him out at the rectory, she makes one last try.

"Do you like being a priest?" she asks.

"No," he says. "But I am one. And that's that." He gets out of the car and looks in at her. He wants to say, *I love you,* but instead he says, "What can I tell you? I'm doomed."

So she makes up her mind. This is it. This is the end.

✝

Father LeBlanc kneels beside Father Moriarty's bed—it's the easiest way to talk with him now—and leans in close.

"Have you ever been tempted to leave the priesthood, Father?"

"Every day," Father Moriarty says.

"Can I ask?"

"Ask."

"If you really doubt God's existence, how can you be a priest? I mean, you say, 'God, if there is a God.'"

"Give me a break," Father Moriarty says. "For that matter, give God a break."

"If there is a God."

"Look," Father Moriarty says, "if you want to leave the priesthood, leave. And if you want to stay, stay. But don't drag me into it."

"I think . . . I think I don't love God. He crushes the life out of me."

Father Moriarty presses his lips together so that he will not say, *Oh, fuck off!* This is one of those moments when your heart turns to ice and you can't breathe and you know you must say the right thing. He has spent a lifetime dreading these moments. How is he supposed to know what to say? What he needs is some kind of spiritual radar that can track the crazy flight of the Holy Ghost, if there is a Holy Ghost. It's all hopeless. He sighs.

"The first commandment, Paul. 'I am the Lord thy God. Thou shalt not have strange gods before me.'"

"Yes?"

"You've created yourself a false god. And you worship him. And you're right, he crushes the life out of you."

"Yes?"

"And he's *you.*"

Father Moriarty closes his eyes to rest them for a second, but he is unable to go on. Father LeBlanc continues to kneel by the bedside. He had been hoping for salvation and this is what he gets.

†

Jake is riding deep into the night, and he hasn't even gotten on his motorcycle yet. He has taken a couple uppers, a couple downers, and he's smoked some grass. Now the purple people eaters have begun to kick in and he has this riding sensation, the feel of the road shooting up through his legs, his crotch all sweaty and nice, and his arms vibrating to the pulse of the tires on the macadam. He closes his eyes and nods off for a while. He's sitting on a rock overlooking the beach where Father LeBlanc used to have picnics with his blond girlfriend, but it's like he's riding his bike and the night is getting darker all the time. He sleeps, and after a while he wakes up and hears the waves beating on the rocks, which sounds just great, and then he nods off again. This is the life. He thinks of Mandy. She was a real cool girl. He would never of wanted her to die.

It's not his fault.

†

Annaka Malley is in Boston, but she will return for the weekend, and Father LeBlanc thinks about her all the time. He is in love with her, he must tell her this, it may be his last chance. This past weekend was a disaster. He was hung up on trying to choose between God and Anna Kathryn and he ended up with neither. And now he has become—

according to Tom Moriarty—an idolater. Of himself, apparently. This is the stunning thing: that he worships himself. How can this be, since he detests himself? And he detests the God who makes him feel this way. Can it be true that all this time he's been worshiping a false God? Made in his own image and likeness? Well, he's capable of any degree of delusion, he knows that. Nonetheless he says mass, he preaches, he forces himself to get through the week. The happy idolater.

Now it is Saturday morning and she doesn't come. She doesn't come in the afternoon, either. She doesn't call to leave a message. She doesn't come on Sunday.

God is telling him something. God is reminding him that, whether he likes it or not, that he is a priest: Reform your life, do penance, love God alone.

But he loves Anna Kathryn.

He phones her in Boston. He phones her at the beach. He leaves messages at both places. No response. Late Sunday night he drives to her house and knocks at the door. Nobody home.

The next morning he wakes at five-thirty, sweaty and still tired after a night of terrible dreams he cannot remember. He throws on his running clothes and heads off down Church Lane toward the beach. The water is like a steel plate, he could walk on it almost, there are practically no waves at all. He stops for a minute to stare out at the horizon. He starts up then and increases his pace until he's running flat out, until he is exhausted and his mouth tastes bitter. He returns home for meditation and mass.

After mass he is walking across the parking lot to the rectory when he meets the postman, who calls out to him, a friend, and hands him a batch of catalogs and a few letters. On top is one from Annaka. He opens it there in the parking lot. It reads, "Dear Paul, It's done and I'm sorry. Forgive me, but you are incapable of happiness and

I'm incapable of living without it. I wish you well." It is signed Anna Kathryn.

He goes inside and drops the letter on his bed. He doesn't bother to change his clothes. Still dressed in his clerics, he walks slowly down to the beach, deserted at this hour, and he looks out over the water, which is beginning to get a little choppy. Far out to sea there is a black cloud, growing. A storm is bearing down on them—an enraged archangel, he thinks—but it won't strike for a while yet. There is still time.

He will swim straight out and see how far he can go. He can always turn back. He's a good swimmer.

He takes off his shoes and socks and tosses them back on the sand. He looks around and sees nobody in sight, so he takes off his shirt and trousers, folds them neatly, and puts them up on the sand. He has on only his T-shirt and undershorts. He dips his fingers in the water—it is cold, cold—and he makes the sign of the cross.

He is just going for a swim. That's all.

He wades into the icy water, and without a pause, he takes the plunge. He surfaces a good distance out, shakes the hair from his eyes, and concentrates on swimming out to the horizon. When I get there, he thinks, I'll turn around. The important thing is to do it.

He swims strongly and with determination and he does not think.

# SEVEN

FATHER LEBLANC HAS LOST ALL SENSE OF TIME. HE swims slowly, powerfully, with no thought of saving strength for his return. The sun has moved higher in the sky, though it is masked now by the storm cloud that continues to grow and darken. He would like to rest for a while, but he keeps on swimming.

The water is gray around him and black below. It smells like the hospital, like sick flesh. And it is icy.

He swims. He is not thinking of Annaka, he merely holds a picture of her in his mind. He should hold there a picture of God, the horizon line toward which he is swimming, but he doesn't. He no longer has any picture of God. His idea of God was simply ego-tism turned inside out, Father Moriarty says, and he is right. It was just another brand of megalomania, extinguishing the self to make it perfect, as if perfection meant getting rid of everything human. He hears the contempt in Father Moriarty's voice: "You've created yourself a false God . . . And he's *you.*"

He is going to swim straight out and then eventually he will turn back. He is not worried about being damned even if he should drown, because he has never believed in damnation.

A wave breaks suddenly against the side of his face, and he gets a mouthful of salty water. He spits, chokes a little, and spits again. "Shit," he says, and for a moment he stops swimming and turns to look back at the shore. He sees the blue pine trees in the far distance, and up closer the maple trees gone brown and yellow, and then the little houses along the shore. For an instant it all falls away: the self-loathing, the self-importance, the self he has been trying all his life to escape. He hears Father Moriarty's exhausted voice: "Why don't you try living just for once." It's a kind of miracle. He is dizzy, confused, then wildly happy. You don't have to hate yourself, you can just live. He has been a love pig and a bore, even to God, and now, when he could start living, he finds himself a mile out to sea.

Suddenly everything seems to go his way. He gets a second wind and breathes deeply, the tide turns in toward shore, and that looming storm cloud finally parts. At that moment the sun breaks through, striking the water and turning it red as wine. He looks up and is blinded by the light. He sees a red sun and a red horizon. He feels suddenly free, and happy, and powerful. He strikes out toward the shore.

†

Father Moriarty is dying at last, he's sure of it. His lungs are filling with fluid, and this is how his mother went. Well, good. He's drowning, which is sort of funny since he has never cared for the beach. He can barely catch his breath. He could go now. It is a choice he has, to surrender. But then there's poor LeBlanc with his life in a mess, an absolute mess, he doesn't know whether he's coming or going. All the women are in love with him, and he's in love with some kind of Aztec god who demands human sacrifice. So Father Moriarty is needed still. He lifts his head a little and clears his throat. "Shit," he says. He will not die yet. But with luck it will be soon.

†

Rose pushes the vacuum cleaner back and forth and sees the pattern of her life, dirty and clean, dirty and clean. She prays to the Virgin to make her pure, but she is thinking less about the Virgin than about Father LeBlanc. She keeps wanting him. She wants his body, naturally, but something more than that. She wants in him whatever it was that he wanted in her, if that makes any sense. It was the miracle. That was why he followed her and looked at her and touched her and got himself up inside her, hard. And when he found that she was just another woman, he went away. He is just another man. She shakes her head and goes on vacuuming. She has been sinning with Nick Pappas lately because at least it keeps her from running after Father LeBlanc. "Hail Mary, full of grace, the Lord is with thee." She forces her way through an entire Hail Mary. What awful things go on in her mind. It's a cesspool. She wants to escape from this place. But she can't escape. She has to stay here for Father Moriarty.

†

Father Moriarty has soiled his bed and lies in the stinking mess hoping the Country Bumpkin will get to him before Rose does. Father LeBlanc is out, of course, at the hospital or somewhere, and by the time he gets back, the house will reek of shit. Maybe he'll get home early and stop by on his way up the stairs.

Well, it's all part of dying, Father Moriarty tells himself, and the shit goes along with it. "He died the way he lived," he says in a whisper, "causing trouble for everybody."

He thinks he hears Rose downstairs. He's not going to pray that Father LeBlanc shows up before she does, but it would be nice if he did. And then he hears Father LeBlanc on the stairs, thundering along as usual; he hears the feet stop at his door, he hears the heavy tap of his knuckles on the wood.

"Come!" Father Moriarty tries to bellow, and though the sound is barely audible outside the door, Father LeBlanc opens it and looks in.

"I wondered if you want . . . oh!" he says, recoiling at the smell, "here, let me change your sheets for you"—he approaches the bed— "and your pajamas, too, I guess."

Father Moriarty is overjoyed to see him, this dumb, holy, tortured, impossible young man. He is wearing his clerical clothes but he is soaking wet. "You look like a drowned rat," Father Moriarty says, and surrenders himself to the indignities that will follow.

Father LeBlanc removes the blanket and checks it for stains. It's okay, so he folds it and lays it on the chair by the bed. "Now," he says, and he lifts the sheet to see the extent of the damage. "I'll have to get those pajamas off first, Father," he says, and he unbuttons the pajama jacket and slips it from under the old priest's shoulders. "And now the pants." He has to lift Father Moriarty with one hand as he slips the pants down with the other. It is easy to do because Father Moriarty is little more than a skeleton now, but it is ghastly because here is this poor defenseless man, naked, soaking in his own shit, and it's humiliating. Nonetheless he does it, and in the process he gets shit all over his hand. "Okay," he says, "very good." Carefully he rolls Father Moriarty's body past the center of the bed. He scrambles the sheets together on this side and uses them to wipe Father Moriarty's buttocks and lower back and, secretly, his own left hand, and then he scrunches them up tight and rolls Father

Moriarty back toward him so that he's lying on this side of the bed with the filthy sheets behind him. "Okay," he says, and for a second he gags. Father Moriarty pretends not to hear him. "All right, okay, now I'll get some warm water and soap in this basin and we'll get you cleaned up."

He does it all. He washes the old priest's body, taking care to remove all the fecal matter from between his legs, around his testicles, even up in his navel. He dries him off, as gently as possible, and he puts baby powder on him so that he won't chafe, and then he gets him back into his pajamas. Father Moriarty lets this happen to him.

"Okay," Father LeBlanc keeps saying. "Okay," and he pulls the clean sheet up to Father Moriarty's chest. "Are you all right? Can I get you anything?"

"You're a good man, Paul," Father Moriarty says.

"I'm leaving," Father LeBlanc says. "I'm going to leave the priesthood."

"I know."

"You were right about the first commandment. Having false gods."

"I know."

"I'm going to try living just for once."

"Paul," Father Moriarty says, "on your wrist. You've got a little smudge of shit right there."

†

Dr. Forbes is early for lunch, and his sister, who keeps house for him, is not sure what to make of this.

"Are you all right?" she asks.

"I'll sit here"—he sits down in the breakfast nook—"and wait for you to get the lunch."

She lifts the lid on the soup to make sure it's at simmer, not boil. Fresh vegetable. Her own. Very healthful. "You're not having a drink? Good," she says, because whether he drinks or not, she can never let the subject alone.

"I'm getting old."

"You're already old. You've been old for years now."

"I mean I'm beginning to feel it."

"Well, you should. You're old."

She gets out the plates and the bowls and cuts two thick slices of eight-grain bread.

"It's that young priest, the French one," Dr. Forbes says.

"LeBlanc. What about him?"

"I drove him back to the church today. From the beach. He was soaking wet."

"Maybe he'd been swimming."

"Of course he'd been swimming. But it was the middle of the morning, and what priest goes swimming then? In his underwear. Besides, he was half dead, and he could barely walk. If I didn't know better . . ."

She doesn't ask. She ladles out the soup and takes it into the dining room. "It's soup," she says, and waits.

He seats her at the head of the table and seats himself at the opposite end.

"If I didn't know better . . ."

But again she doesn't ask.

". . . I'd think he was trying to drown himself."

"Perhaps he was."

He expected astonishment from her, or surprise at least. He's a little disappointed.

"Maybe he's in love," she says. "Or perhaps both. They're compatible instincts. Suicide. Love."

"What are you talking about?"

"He's a very good-looking man, is Father LeBlanc. He's very sexy."

Dr. Forbes stares at his sister. She is a maiden lady without experience and without any shadows on her life. She is famously a good woman. So what is this new and startling prurience he sees in her? He tastes the soup, which is delicious.

Life and people remain a mystery to him.

†

Annaka Malley is a One L at Suffolk Law, and like all the others, she is overwhelmed by courses in civil procedure, contracts, torts, and legal research. Everybody says that if she can survive the first year, the rest is a breeze, but she can't help noticing that the Two L students seem every bit as harried as she is. She uses the work, though, to keep from thinking of Father LeBlanc. She knows she will be able to think about him eventually without longing and without any pain, but right now she's trying to keep busy. She has put the beach house in the hands of a Realtor, and she does not drive up there on weekends.

She is out of his life for good.

She is too old to take on Father LeBlanc's neuroses. She's got all she can handle with her own. He sends her letters all the time, with jokes in them, with upbeat funny stories, all in an attempt to prove that he can be happy. And he sends her those damned Hallmark happy cards. Jokes are not happy, she tells him. Hallmark is not happy. Happy comes from inside. Give me a chance, he says. What's to lose? Give me a break, she says. But he does not give her a break. This is a siege. He is well fortified—with charm, with looks, with a new determination to live his own life and to live it with her—and he is not going away until the city falls. It's a siege, he says. Love and war. Think Helen of Troy.

Annaka Malley, at thirty, is too old to start a new life with a new man with a whole new set of idiosyncrasies. Not to mention her old worry about commitment. Although, with Paul LeBlanc, it is precisely commitment that she feels. She loves him still, even though half the time she'd like to kill him, and she knows he is a man she can marry. She knew that the first moment she saw him in church, and hard as she has tried to crush it out, that conviction remains. Romantic nonsense, she tells herself. Helen of Troy.

It's all over with Father LeBlanc. She is out of his life for good. For his own good and for hers.

But how difficult it is. Like interrupting the act of love.

"If in doubt, choose life," Father Moriarty said to her, and God knows, she would . . . she will . . . if she's ever given the chance. But at the moment life is law school, and Father LeBlanc keeps hovering on the edge of her consciousness, smiling.

†

Father LeBlanc is driving down to Boston. He plans to take her to a nice little Italian restaurant in the North End and say, "Marry me."

He explains it all. He has applied for laicization. He will be examined by a monsignor appointed by the bishop especially for his case. "My case," he says, "don't you love the sound of it?" It could take up to a year, but he doesn't mention that. He says:

"Marry me."

"Why—when I won't even answer your letters—why would you think I'd want to marry you?"

"Not *want* to marry me. Just be willing." He gives her a smile he thinks is lecherous, and she can't help smiling back because it's a smile of pure innocence. "Besides, you do answer my letters," he says.

"Very few, and only out of charity."

"See?" he says. "You love me. And I can be happy. Look at me, I'm a happy guy."

"Well, I'm One L and I haven't got time for marriage. Or for being happy."

"I'm gonna get a teaching job. Latin. I've applied to high schools all over Boston and I'm sure to get a job."

"Good for you."

"And I'll be laicized soon. All I have to do is wait for the papers."

"Don't do it for me," she says.

"It's not for you. It's for me."

"Good."

"*I'm* for you."

"What's that supposed to mean?"

"Use your fine legal mind, Anna Kathryn. Can't you see?" He puts her through the slow ordeal of his smile. "*I'm* your vocation. *I'm* your fate."

She smiles finally, and he says, "Now, let's have a little chorus of 'Cry Me a River.' Can you do Streisand?"

†

Father Moriarty has soiled his bed again. Mrs. Schwartz will be along any time now and will clean him up, wash him and dry him and start him out once more with clean sheets. What can the point of all this be?

Perhaps he is being cleansed in some special, hideous way.

Perhaps he is a lesson to the others: Rose and Father LeBlanc and Mrs. Schwartz and who else? But what would the lesson be, please?

Perhaps he is part of some cosmic joke.

Perhaps he *is* the joke.

Perhaps human nature is such that matter and energy in the end can produce only this outpouring of shit.

He's getting a headache.

Perhaps he is an opportunity for the others to exercise patience, a *memento mori,* a threat, a promise . . . if there is a God, if God cares at all.

Perhaps this is an act of love.

"Well, here we are," Mrs. Schwartz says, as she swings into the room with energy and good humor. "I think we could use a little bath, couldn't we, and some nice clean sheets." She places her hand on his forehead for a moment, nods, and says, "Good, you're very good," and sets up shop to give him a bath.

She works with efficiency and dispatch. In no time she has the bed stripped down to the rubber sheet and Father Moriarty stripped down to his skin and bones, and she is talking happily about the movie she and Mr. Schwartz watched last night—"too much violence but a very interesting story about a war with aliens called Wookies and so forth. They talk a lot about the Force. May the Force be with you, they say. And Alec Guinness, no less." Special effects in movies have begun to interest her almost more than anything else, she says. "Morphing, they call it. And miniaturization, of course, and all kinds of miraculous things they can do with computers now. The human mind is a great thing," she says. "And machines, of course. It's really the machines that do it all."

So he is washed and dried and powdered and put together again for the remainder of the afternoon. He cannot last much longer. He knows that and she knows that. He will not have many more opportunities. "Mrs. Schwartz," he says. He can barely get out the words, and she has to lean down and listen carefully. "I love you," he says.

Mrs. Schwartz pulls back, surprised. "That'll be quite enough of that," she says, and picks up her handbag and her satchel. At the door she pauses and says, "I give equal care to all my patients, regardless of race, creed, or color, you should know that by now." Looking at him, though, she softens and adds, "I hope you have a nice day." She goes down the stairs and immediately comes back up. "The Force be with you," she says, greatly pleased.

†

Father LeBlanc has been summoned to the Kremlin for his examination. The bishop's residence looks exactly the same as it did two years ago, except it is darker, gloomier, and as he sits in the guest parlor, Father LeBlanc begins to cough. He feels as if he is inhaling all the dust of the past two years. He clears his throat and coughs again. Nerves.

A young priest, a seminarian perhaps, appears at the door. He is short and fat, balding already, and he wears thick glasses. He nods to Father LeBlanc and gestures toward the corridor. "The first door," he says, frowning, and then startles Father LeBlanc with a broad smile. "Good luck!" he says.

Monsignor Glynn comes from behind his desk to shake Father LeBlanc's hand.

"How's my friend?" he asks.

"Father Moriarty's not doing very well. It won't be long, I think."

"No, I meant you, Paul. How are you doing?"

"Well, I'm here. For my examination."

"It's called a *scrutatio*, formally, a deposition. Interesting term, no?" Monsignor Glynn goes back behind his desk. "Have a seat. So you've reached the end of the line. Well, it happens. I've been assigned to be your interrogator, so here, put your hand on this Bible and I'll take down your answers longhand."

Father LeBlanc looks at him. "Interrogator?"

"It's just a term," Monsignor Glynn says. "We're dealing with Rome here, Father. I'm the interrogator. You're the priest-petitioner. These papers are official documents." He looks at him. "Got it? I didn't make this stuff up. And let's not forget, you're the one who's asking to be laicized."

"Right."

"'Reduced to the lay state.' Another term they use. 'Reduced.'"

Father LeBlanc reminds himself he is doing this because it must be done. You don't walk away from a fifteen-year commitment by saying, *Fuck it, I'm moving on,* though right now he would like to.

"Ready?"

For more than an hour Father LeBlanc sits with his right hand on the Bible—the Douay version, no surprise—and answers ques-

tions about whether his parents married for love or out of obliga-
tion, whether he was a wanted or unwanted baby, whether they sug-
gested the priesthood to him or he chose it himself. He answers
truthfully and contradicts himself and answers again. He doesn't
know. He is not sure. He cannot say. Monsignor Glynn hunches
uncomfortably over his desk and writes everything down in his cu-
riously small and perfect handwriting.

"Why does this have to be handwritten?" Father LeBlanc asks.
"This is going to take forever."

"You've been a priest for how long? A few hours more doesn't
seem too much to ask."

"Sorry," Father LeBlanc says.

"Okay, let's go."

"But who could answer these questions?" Father LeBlanc interrupts again. "This whole process is designed to prove I never really
had a vocation, that somehow I was forced into this. But you're not
going to make me say that. I was *not* forced into the priesthood. I *did*
understand fully what I was doing. I *chose* it. For the wrong reasons,
obviously, but I chose it."

Monsignor Glynn is tired. He sits back and assumes a look of
patience. "And what were those reasons, pray?"

"I felt I could and therefore should and therefore did."

"It sounds like a formula."

"Pure reason. Nothing else."

"No love for God involved?"

"A false God." Silence. "Love of my own virtue." He laughs
suddenly, ridiculously. "I was a love pig."

Monsignor Glynn looks at him and shakes his head. He seems
to mouth the words, "love pig." "Let's go on," he says. "Let's get
through this."

They cover masturbation, fornication, adultery. No surprises there. "Sins with men?"

"No men," Father LeBlanc says.

"Ah." Monsignor Glynn takes out his handkerchief and mops his brow. Father LeBlanc laughs, thinking he means to be funny.

"Yes?" Monsignor Glynn is puzzled.

"No. I mean we're nervous. Or at least I am."

"All right. Now, about these women."

"Woman. One. Only once. As you know."

"This is official, Paul. Officially, I know nothing. Would you call it a brief affair?"

"A mistake. A self-indulgent mistake. My fault, completely."

"Lust."

"Yes."

"Well, it happens. No further harm done?"

"No further harm?"

Monsignor Glynn looks at him as if he is truly stupid. "Pregnancy? A child?" He pauses. "An abortion?"

"Good God, no!" Incredibly, Father LeBlanc has never thought of this, and now he is overwhelmed with relief and gratitude. And then panic. "No!"

"Well, it happens. You've been lucky."

"I was. I am."

Monsignor Glynn mops his brow again. They finish with sex and go on to questions of priestly duties.

"You were sent to Our Lady of Victories for a reason, it says here."

"I was trouble."

"Busing. Integration. Birth control. The usual." He looks up with what seems to be a smile. "These things mattered at the time."

"Are we almost done?"

"Patience. Patience. Do you mind if I have a cigarette?" He lights it without waiting for an answer. "Now, matters of faith."

Father LeBlanc groans.

"What? Faith is a problem? You've lost your faith?"

"I don't know what faith is."

"Faith is believing where we cannot prove. It's pretty basic, Father. It's ultimately why you're here." He clarifies. "In the priesthood. In this room. Now."

"I don't know about faith. I have *hope*. That seems enough for the time being."

"And the love of God?" Monsignor Glynn asks.

"I'll have to find out who God is. Meanwhile, I don't want to love God, any God, I want to love someone."

"You go too far." Monsignor Glynn's voice is suddenly the voice of God, the God Father LeBlanc knows so well. "You go too far."

"Yes," Father LeBlanc says.

Another two hours pass and they are done. Monsignor Glynn sees him to the door, places his heavy hand on Father LeBlanc's shoulder, and says in a gentle voice, "God bless."

On the stairs, he says, "By the way, if you haven't seen *Jaws,* see it as soon as you can. It's a hoot."

†

Rose has dropped by to spend a few minutes with Father Moriarty. She left the Clam Box early, before her shift was over, because there's very little night business at this time of year and Sal doesn't really care.

"I stopped by to see that you're okay," she says. She sits down in the chair next to the bed and leans in to him. "How are you doing?"

Father Moriarty does something with his eyes that evidently means *Okay*.

"Do you have water? Do you need anything to drink?"

Okay again.

"I'm feeling really bad about the things I've done, especially the thing with Father LeBlanc. I'm the guilty one, to tell you the truth, it's my fault that he came to me like that, he never would of except that I wanted him so much. I'm the one to blame."

She shoots him a quick glance but she can't tell what he's thinking.

"It used to be life was simple. Mandy was such a good kid, and so pretty and smart, and she got good grades in school and everything. I had my weaknesses, you know, like sex, but I went to confession and I prayed to the Virgin and I got by all right. I mean, I fell, but mostly I was doing all right. And then Mandy began going around with that rough crowd, and Jake and everything, and the motorcycles. It all began with him. He was the start of it, that long hair and filthy jeans, and the ring in his nose and everything else. He was the start. And he killed my Mandy. Not with the motorcycle only, but with the drugs and everything. She would never of taken drugs if she hadn't got involved with him. After she died, it was never the same. It was like I was a crazy woman, and having sex was like getting even with God, you know? Even with a priest. I knew what I was doing and I did it and I haven't had a minute's peace since."

She sits back and looks at her hands, folded on the bed.

"So I guess I've got to forgive him," she says. "Jake, I mean."

Father Moriarty moves his hand so that his fingers rest against hers. He tries to nod his head, *Yes*.

She looks up at him and smiles.

"I came to cheer you up, and I'm probably making you want to drop dead." She looks at him. "Sorry, I shouldn't have said that, but you know what I mean."

"Are you okay?" she asks.

"Are you gonna be okay?" she asks again.

She sits on the edge of the bed and lowers her forehead until it touches his. "Okay?"

"I'll go now," she says.

"Yes," he says, a croaking sound. There is a smile on his lips.

†

Jake is full of coke tonight and feeling really good. He's had enough down times to last the rest of his life, so it's way cool to be in control again, the man in charge. No more guilt shit for him. No more asking Rose for forgiveness. No more nothing. It's great to be sitting on this bike with the handlebars vibrating in your grip and your crotch going ringadingading and the cold air like ice in your hair and your eyes and your throat. This feels wild. This feels really wild.

He comes to a turn in the highway, not quite a hairpin turn but tricky enough anyhow, and he leans into the curve—he's flying almost parallel to the road now, the side of his left shoe burns on the macadam—and then he's upright again, and the curve is behind him, and he laughs, a barking sound, because he did it so cool, flirting with death this way.

It's all part of his new plan: no drugs tomorrow or the day after or the rest of his freaking life. Just drugs today. Every day.

He speeds up as he approaches the next curve. Why not!

†

Father LeBlanc is a new man. He is more like his old self, when he first came to Our Lady of Victories. He sings in the house and he plays basketball with the kids, and he is great with the students in his evening class and with the vets at the hospital and with nearly everybody.

Dr. Forbes mentions this to his sister, who merely raises her eyebrows, keeping her thoughts to herself. Rose mentions it to Nick Pappas, who gives Father LeBlanc his highest compliment: "He's a good shit." Father Moriarty notices and says nothing.

Father LeBlanc's laicization papers have gone to Rome, so now it is only a matter of time until he is out. Free. Reduced to the lay state. Meanwhile he is still a priest, and a good one.

†

Rose is driving home after her morning at the church rectory. Father Moriarty cannot last much longer; he is a breathing corpse, a skeleton, and he has been like this for months. Rose doesn't feel good about leaving him alone, because he worries her. But then everything worries her these days, or upsets her. Father LeBlanc has told her he's leaving the priesthood. Jake, whom she's trying to forgive, is unforgivable. Sal is getting divorced and has given her notice on the apartment above the Clam Box. Everything is falling apart. You can't depend on anything. She thinks she may go to California once Father Moriarty dies. Drive out, see the country, get a real job. Make something of herself. Or, who knows, maybe stay here at the beach and move in with Nick Pappas, who says he loves her.

As she pauses at the corner where Church Lane intersects with the shore drive, her car stalls. She turns off the ignition and sits looking ahead. Gray skies. Gray ocean. A gray life. Her mind is a tangle of worry and frustration and anger. She has a pain in her forehead and a pain in her heart and, to tell the truth, an ache in her groin. She lowers her head to the steering wheel to rest for a second.

She rests, her hands in her lap.

And suddenly she is aware of something in the car with her. She is so certain of its presence that she does not even turn around. Nor is she frightened. With her eyes still closed, she raises her head, she puts her hands on the steering wheel, she waits. She can feel it—him—breathing on her neck.

This is death, of course, but she had thought death would be more frightening.

He puts his arms around her and holds her close, softly. She is filled with a long warmth, sexual but much more than sexual, because all her bones seem flooded with light and there is a soft stirring in the air surrounding her and she gives herself up to this embrace. It lasts how long? She doesn't know. But when he withdraws his arms, she is still Rose and she is still sitting in her battered old car at the corner of Church Lane and the beach road and she is alone.

She opens her eyes, leans back against the seat, and sees it has begun to snow. Large perfect flakes fall out of the sky, melt against the windshield, whirl in small eddies along the street. All her worries fall away, the guilt, the ugliness, the hate.

This embrace, she realizes, is a premonition. She does not want to die, especially not now, but if it's time, well then it's time. She starts the car and drives toward home.

She makes a cup of tea, Constant Comment, and waits for death. But death does not come, and instead she is filled once more with the feeling of that embrace, the light in her bones, a kind of ecstasy. Like sex but even better. She sits by the window and listens to the sea pounding against the boats in the harbor. The snow rages and whitens at the glass. And she waits, ready. She nods off and wakes and nods off again.

When dawn comes, she is still sitting by the window. The snow has stopped, the storm has passed. This will be a clear winter day.

She opens her eyes and sees the white sun on the black water, and deliberately, afraid it may be gone forever, she summons the feeling of that embrace, and miraculously, it comes. She feels the warmth and the force of it, and at last, she knows the meaning of that embrace. It is not about dying, but living.

She thinks of Father Moriarty. She must tell him this, but in the end it matters too much to talk about, so she tells no one.

†

It is a cold winter morning with soft yellow light, and there is frost on the windowpane. Father Moriarty opens his eyes to this dazzle and realizes all at once that it is time. He can go at last because he is all done here. Later in the day, Father LeBlanc's laicization papers arrive.

Father LeBlanc will be fine.

Father LeBlanc has God in him like a stinger.

†

Nearly the last thing Father Moriarty senses is the smell of pine trees under melting snow. How wonderful that spring is coming. And now he is aware of the low cry of night birds and the soughing sound of wind through the trees. His senses reel because it is all so delicious. He is dying at last, alone, sleeping perhaps, though in his sleep he feels himself borne up effortlessly, by something, by someone. He thins out into circumambient air, but as he does, he reaches up and

216

his hand fades in darkness and another hand grasps his. This new and comfortable dark is more light than humankind can bear. It is enough, he knows, it will suffice.

†

Father LeBlanc phones Anna Kathryn and is in the middle of leaving a long message when she picks up the phone. He has said that Father Moriarty is dead at last and that he'll be buried two days from now and will she come to the funeral. Hello, hello, she says, of course she'll come to the funeral, poor wonderful Father Moriarty, and how are you doing yourself, are you all right? Sadder than I might have thought, he says, now that I'm nearly a layman.

There is silence on the line.

"My papers came," he says. "Once I sign them, it's official. I'm out."

More silence.

"I could even marry," he says, and when he hears nothing from her end of the line, he says, "if I had someone who was willing, I mean." He is in trouble, he has said the wrong thing, and he begins to talk fast. "But this isn't the time to talk about me. I shouldn't be talking about me at all. I'm not. I mean, I am but I don't mean to." And it comes to him clearly that if Anna Kathryn should break down someday and marry him, he'll be in trouble in just this way for the rest of his life. "I've got to go," he says. "I'm pleased you'll come to the funeral."

†

Anna Kathryn wrings her hands like a heroine in a soap opera. She paces from the living room to the kitchen of her small apartment, and she is actually wringing her hands. Like a bad actress, she thinks. And then, since this is real and she is further from acting than she has ever been, she wonders if perhaps this is how people behave when they're told they'll be led out at dawn tomorrow and shot.

This is against her wishes. This is against her will. She does not want to see Paul LeBlanc and get all that craziness stirred up again, and she certainly does not want to marry him, so why does she feel she will and she must?

"I do not love him," she says aloud, acting. "I do not want to see him." And she wrings her hands. "I will not see him. I will not love him." Et cetera, et cetera, she concludes, a lawyer giving up.

Very early on the day of the funeral, she drives north to Our Lady of Victories parish for perhaps the last time.

†

Winter is not yet over, and though the ground is still frozen, a grave has been dug for Father Moriarty's burial. The day is clear and the air is cold, but at least there is no wind, and the pale sun shows signs of warming things up. There is a large crowd for the funeral.

Father LeBlanc has only to sign his papers and he will become a layman, but he has not signed them yet. He has asked permission to bury Father Moriarty first. It is the last and the best thing he can do as a priest, and he owes it to Father Moriarty, he tells Monsignor Glynn. Monsignor Glynn agrees.

Now they are burying him. It is a Catholic burial, a ritual of departure, and emotion is kept to the edge of things. Monsignor Glynn has preached a homily on death and resurrection, and Father LeBlanc has said the funeral mass and led the congregation out through the snow to the cemetery, and he has read the prayers for the burial of a priest. There are perhaps a hundred people at the grave. Everyone who knew Father Moriarty seems to have come out in the snow for this last good-bye. Father Moriarty has no family left, and so after the coffin is lowered into the grave, it is Monsignor Glynn who drops the first clod of earth upon it. The hard dull sound echoes in the empty air. Father LeBlanc blesses the coffin one last time, and though he has not intended to say anything, he does.

"Father Moriarty was an exemplary priest. He lived a life of faith and love, of charity and justice, and whatever he touched he sanctified." He feels tears coming and concludes quickly, "He was— in some incomprehensible way—a saint."

The sun appears briefly as most of the congregation begins to drift away. A few people stay on to shake hands with Monsignor Glynn and Father LeBlanc and join them for coffee in the rectory parlor. The tiny room is packed with people, and they drift out to the corridor and even to the kitchen. They all know Father LeBlanc is leaving the priesthood and they are all uncomfortable about it, but he moves among them easily, greeting each of them warmly, saying a word or two and moving on to the next. He kisses Rose on the cheek and shakes Nick Pappas's hand. This is awkward for everybody because Father LeBlanc, still dressed in clerics, seems very much a priest. He, on the other hand, has never felt so much at ease.

Anna Kathryn approaches him at last. Only Dr. Forbes and his sister remain behind her; others stand around in small groups. Father LeBlanc has seen her at the funeral mass and again at the burial, and he has prayed that she would stay for coffee in the rectory.

And here she is. She moves forward and shakes his hand firmly. The Forbeses look at the couple and then look at each other. Something is happening here. Even at their great age, they recognize the signs.

"I'm sorry about Father's death," she says, and Father LeBlanc holds her hand a second too long. She is about to pull away, but instead she grips his hand more firmly and then, awkward, they look up at each other. They are locked for a moment in this ridiculous handshake, blood pulsing together in their palms, and he smiles and she smiles. Suddenly, inappropriately, they laugh.

"I have to go sign things," he says, and backs away from her. "Can I see you outside, at your car?" She nods and he goes upstairs.

Later, the guests finish their coffee and say their good-byes and drift off to their cars. Nobody is left except Monsignor Glynn, who feels suddenly very old and very tired. Paul LeBlanc comes down the stairs. He is wearing gray slacks and a black turtleneck and a Red Sox jacket. He looks young and handsome and suddenly very shy. Monsignor Glynn, who has been waiting for him, gives him a hug and a good hard rap on the back and says, "God bless, Paul." And Paul LeBlanc says, "God bless" in return.

"Will you be back for your stuff?" Monsignor Glynn asks.

"Tonight."

"We'll have a drink."

Paul LeBlanc goes out to the parking lot. He can see his breath in the air, and he exhales an attempt at a smoke ring. Anna Kathryn is standing by her car. She is wearing a brown wool coat and a matching hat and boots, and she is smiling at him. She looks breathtaking, and for a moment he actually cannot catch his breath. His heart races.

"You waited," he says.

"You bet."

"So, you're giving in to fate?"

She makes a formal pronouncement: "I have been sent by God to rescue you. From yourself."

He laughs, as he was meant to laugh, and then he gives her that wicked, innocent smile.

"And I accept my fate," he says.

"As you should," she says, "and be grateful for it."

They stand there silent for a moment—a challenge—and then they shake hands on it. The sun does not come out, nor does a bird call from the woods, nor do they fall into each other's arms. It is a bleak, cold, cloudy morning, unpromising, with snow expected in the afternoon. It is perfect, in its way.